DREAMS

Visionary creations of the imagination.
Strongly desired goals or purposes.
Something to fully satisfy a wish.
A condition or achievement that is longed for; an aspiration.

Dreams come from the Heart
… as the "Voice" of the Soul.

Written in loving memory
of my daughter Kimberly Wood.
Kim was a prolific writer up to the day before her death,
December 22, 1999,

and she encouraged me to:

Write with Passion
For Self
For Sanity
For Fun
Forever!

Everett R. Wood
Fort Collins, Colorado
February 2017

Chasing Dreams

by

Everett R. Wood

First Edition

ISBN 978-0-692-87579-7

Acknowledgements

With an apology to my English teachers over the years, I wish to acknowledge any imperfections or errors that remained after my three personal reviews and corrections.

Special thanks to my son, Barry Wood for his help and expertise in creating the cover for this book. To my son, Gregory for his computer skills in preparing this story for publication. And, to my daughter, Kelly Ford for her constant encouragement.

The final review of this book (my second literary effort*) was handled by professional editor, Colleen Brennan and my daughter-in-law, Cindy Fravel, to whom I express my unending gratitude.

Next, I wish to acknowledge the special understanding given me by all members of my family and close friends, of the obvious obsession I had for this novel and the almost reclusive nature that I entered into during its writing and preparation for publishing.

* My 1st book, published in 2006, was "Broken Dreams":
A tale of How the Wild West Turned a Frontier Doctor's Dream's to Ashes.

Story Background

This is a historical, fictionalized tale based on family history and events as related to me by my father, Russell W. Wood Sr., and several of his twelve brothers and sisters. The story is about their maternal grandfather and grandmother, Michael Myers and Philomene Gardner, who were my great-grandparents.

Michael's last name was spelled differently throughout his life. In the family Bible, it was spelled "Myres." The U.S. Army spelled it either "Meyers" or "Myers." For the sake of consistency, I've used the spelling "Myers" throughout the book.

A great deal of research went into developing this story to ensure as much historical accuracy as possible. However, the knowledgeable reader may recognize errors made or liberties taken with some events, names, dates, or places. It is my desire that those readers forgive my inaccuracies and enjoy it for what it is – a story of possible realities based on known family history. I further hope the story will prompt the reader to think of the scores of other unknown pioneers who helped open the American West with their own turbulent and exciting adventures.

CHAPTER 1
"TAKE YOUR STAND AND MAKE YOUR MARK!"

The year was 1836. The military was converging on the small village of Vicerstrophen, Baden in the loose confederacy of Germany. While they moved from home to home throughout the village, Michael Myers, the second-born son of Almeric and Kristen Myers, lay hiding in the nearby forest.

His older brother Everhart first became aware of the military's presence as he was returning from the fields that surrounded the village. He hastened home to alert his mother and father, and especially his brother Michael.

The family knew that Michael had recently joined an underground freedom fighting group of young men with revolutionary ideals. The dramatist and novelist Karl Gutzkow was the pioneer of this social movement.

He was also the leader of the Young Germany social reform and literary movement, which opposed Romanticism and sought to incite others to fight for social and political justice. These young Freedom Fighters did everything they could to oppose the rules, regulations, taxes, and recent laws the king had placed on all inhabitants of the loose confederacy of Germany. The Freedom Fighters had as their motto: "Take Your Stand and Make Your Mark!" Additionally, they fervently supported the four freedoms:

1. Freedom of speech/expression
2. Freedom of religion/belief
3. Freedom from want
4. Freedom from fear

This movement had begun a number of years earlier, as a result of Napoleon Bonaparte's successes in bringing some semblance of freedom to the nearby communities in France just across the border from Baden, Germany.

The ancient village of Vicerstrophen in the territory of Baden was a small farming hamlet in the southwestern part of the loose confederacy of Germany. Most families were very poor and worked the surrounding farms as serfs. The Myers family was no different in this regard. They received a small payment for their tedious labor, but most of what they received went back to the landowner for the "privilege" of farming his land.

Michael was a muscular boy of 15 whose strength came from engaging in heavy physical work. Schooling was difficult and often interrupted by essential farm duties. Unlike his brother Everhart, Michael was fortunate in being able to attend a small school in the nearby village of Freiburg. Public schools had begun to spring up only a few years previously as the importance of education gained popularity throughout the confederacy.

Michael and Everhart's father was a man of narrow convictions and one with a firm and inflexible regard for

German family traditions. His mother, on the other hand, possessed a quiet air of authority with rare warmth and was one who encouraged personal thought and education. While Michael enjoyed his schooling very much and preferred it to his farm duties, he particularly enjoyed the company of the other boys with whom he came in contact. This proved to be healthy but dangerous – healthy from the standpoint of expanding his views of life but dangerous from its influence and its disruptive effect on him and his beliefs about life.

He became enthralled with the young Freedom movement arising throughout the area and devoted every spare moment that he could in support of it.

The government, fearing a full-fledged revolution on its hands, sent troops into the area to seek out the most outspoken and active members of the movement. When discovered, these perpetrators were taken into custody. Although Michael was quite young, his personal safety was jeopardized by his involvement and numerous previous actions taken in his belief of the Freedom movement's principles.

Most recently, he and his Freedom Fighter comrades-in-arms had seriously disrupted a meeting in a neighboring village. Things had gotten completely out of hand with name-calling and rock-throwing. During the commotion, an important public building had caught fire, threatening the entire community. Previously, there had been other incidents of public disorder, protest marches, and disruptive shouting by the Freedom Fighters throughout the surrounding villages. But none had escalated or become as violent or dangerous to the general public as this latest action.

Now Michael lay on the cold damp ground in the forest outside his home village watching the military carefully moving from home to home. He realized that not only had he put himself at risk through his participation with the Freedom Fighters, but he had also put his family in danger.

Lying there in the quiet of the forest, he became aware he must somehow relieve his family of this problem he had created.

As darkness descended, he made one quick, cautious trip to the nearby field to obtain a turnip and a few carrots to cure his hunger pangs. He was alert to the danger of leaving the forest he knew so well, and so he remained there overnight and well into the next day. As morning broke, he watched the soldiers stir in the camp they had set up within a few hundred meters of Michael's home. Fear of the unknown knotted and writhed in his stomach and up came last evening's turnip and carrot supper.

The soldiers made one last sweeping check around the village homes and surrounding areas. They moved toward Michael's hiding place in the forest.

He felt the whisper of terror run though him as they came closer – so close he thought he could no longer escape their discovery. He prayed to be saved by a last-minute miracle.

CHAPTER 2

FEAR, NEVER FELT BEFORE

Michael lay as still as a blade of grass on a windless day, as the soldiers came closer. Suddenly, someone shouted from a distance. The soldiers turned to see a man pointing to a distant area of the forest. "Over there! Over there!" the man shouted, pointing to a rustling in the woods, as the soldiers ran quickly across the open fields to investigate.

Meanwhile Michael recognized the shouting man as his brother, Everhart, and suspected the soldiers would find nothing more than a fox out seeking its breakfast. This diversion gave Michael the time to disappear deeper into the forest and await the "all clear" signal his brother would provide.

As he awaited his brother's call, Michael, still cold from sleeping on the forest floor and tired from lack of sleep, contemplated what he could do to protect himself and his family. Like a bolt out of the sky, he knew that leaving home was the only course of action that would save his family from further stress or harm. How and where to go became his immediate concern, for now all across the confederacy similar "roundups" of revolutionary youth dissenters were taking place. No place seemed a safe haven for a young boy on the run.

As Michael pondered his options, he recalled his teacher mentioning a place called "America" in the New World, a country that had recently gained independence from England and where, now, freedom reigned supreme.

His teacher had loaned him Gottfried Duden's book *A Journey to the Western States of North America,* published in 1829. Duden's account of life on a small farm in Missouri sounded idyllic to Michael.

The idea of going to America excited him so much that he thought his mind would explode. Just then, his brother blew the "all clear" signal on his handmade bull horn.

When Michael was sure the military had left the area, he returned home to his mother's open arms. In the evening, he related all the previous activities in which he had been involved. His confession came as a surprise to his parents. His brother shook his head. "How could you put our family and yourself in such danger?" Everhart asked.

The family discussed various alternatives, but none seemed to spare Michael from the long arms of the government should he be caught.

Michael knew he must act quickly. He had no money, and the thought of leaving his parents in their devastating position in life caused Michael to agonize over what to do. His parents depended on the help of their two sons, as they all worked their small piece of land, for their very survival. They resorted to hiding Michael whenever government soldiers were in the area and pleading ignorance when confronted about him by the military.

Weeks passed. One by one, most of the other young agitators in their village and in the surrounding villages were arrested and led to a fate unknown. Fear, like the quick hot touch of the devil, shot through Michael at the thought that any one of his comrades-in-arms might betray him. It became more critical for Michael to spring into action to save himself from prosecution for what the government described as "misguided revolutionary freedom actions … both physical and verbal."

CHAPTER 3
THE ULTIMATE DECISION

Considerable discussion was held every evening in the Myers's household after chores were done. All ideas concerning Michael's safety were discussed in great detail and either discarded or set aside for further thought.

Michael finally made the decision that he would seek his fortune in the America he had heard so much about. He decided that he would leave home as soon as possible to save his family from any reprisals for his personal actions. They all knew from the village gossip that the military had not yet given up on rounding up the dissenting youth. It was only a matter of time before Michael would be identified and apprehended.

The next day, with the blessings of his family and tears from his mother, Michael gathered his few belongings and stuffed them into a burlap bag. He included the book he had been given by his teacher, who had taken a liking to Michael's adventuresome attitude. The book described the wonders of the New World, called the United States of America, and the opportunities offered there.

As the evening sun began to set, Michael huddled in the small kitchen, by the warming fireplace, to both hear and give final words before his departure. His mother, Kristen, was taking his pending departure the hardest. His father, who seemingly understood, grasped the broad shoulders of his youngest son and, with a few hardy pats on the back, wished him great adventures and a better life. His older brother thought him foolhardy to try to escape the long reach of the current government as well as to put himself into further jeopardy or increased danger. He thought his departure would be a definitive admission of his guilt and his involvement with the revolutionary movement.

Although Michael had contemplated and mentally redefined his escape plan many times, there remained numerous unconsidered aspects of the journey. After a final kiss from his mother and two or three more husky slaps on the back by his father, Michael walked with stooped shoulders through the small narrow door held open by his older brother. After walking twenty or thirty steps, Michael turned to wave his last good-bye but found that his brother had already closed the door. Perhaps, Michael thought, to protect the small dwelling from the increasing cold of the early evening.

As Michael took his last look at the place he had lived from birth to his now 15 years of age, his eyes moistened. He recognized that, undoubtedly, this would be the last time he would see his loved ones and the surrounding low mountains he loved and in which he had grown up.

He hurried to the river's edge and to the secret spot where his raft lay hidden in the underbrush. He had built this raft over the previous weeks from scavenged scraps of lumber and fallen tree timbers. He had done most of this work at night so it would not be detected. Only Michael knew of its purpose and its hiding place on the bank of the Harmersbach River.

CHAPTER 4
THE ADVENTURE BEGINS…THE ESCAPE

Michael knew little about where the river flowed, but he hoped it would take him far away from Vicerstrophen and the trouble he had gotten himself into.

He loaded his few belongings onto the loosely formed raft he had constructed and pushed the raft to the water's edge. He paused, staring at the darkness of the river, and decided to await first light before setting off. He felt utterly alone as he lay on the moss-covered bank. Sleep came fitfully.

Dawn was breaking as he awoke with a start. His full consciousness awakened as he heard his name called from a distance. The sound came closer and closer as he tried to identify who was calling.

His good-byes had been said and his mind was made up. So without further thought, he pushed his raft into the river and jumped aboard. The current was swifter than in previous days due to the snow melt in the low mountains that surrounded the area. It made for a quick exit from whatever possible danger lurked from whoever was calling his name through the morning mist. Soon the raft gathered more speed through the rough waters and a number of times bounced off the bank of the river. Not having much knowledge of river crafts, Michael had not provided himself with any steering device, not even a paddle. Nonetheless, he continued to put distance between himself and the voices that now grew fainter. The sound of the water beneath his raft helped muffle the voices and calm his nerves.

By mid-morning, Michael was moving rapidly down the center of the river. Other than the few uncontrollable jolting bounces off the bank, he was happy with his progress. However, the blood and bruising on his hands and arms showed the extent of his attempts to keep his raft from colliding with boulders and fallen trees and to free the raft when it temporarily became lodged.

In the late afternoon, the raft slowed as it floated in the shallow water around one of the larger bends in the river. Michael jumped off and pulled the raft to the bank of the river. There he ate his first meal since leaving home. The loaf of hard bread and the small slice of cheese were no comparison to the hearty meal he knew his mother would be cooking about this time. He guessed he had been floating for about 10 hours without a break. He felt safe, away from harm's way, and decided that, even though much daylight remained, he would not travel any farther that day.

He surveyed the surrounding land but found nothing other than a ripe vegetable field apparently farmed by the folks in the distant house on the hillside. A soft sandy beach and food nearby – what more could a young man ask for? Besides, he was exhausted from the activities and stress of the preceding 24 hours.

He pulled his raft farther up on the sandy beach, ate some vegetables from the nearby field, and stretched out on the cool ground. As the evening stars appeared, sleep came to the young man. Other than the sniffing and barking of a visiting dog shortly after he closed his eyes, Michael slept peacefully through the night.

CHAPTER 5
A SURPRISE ENCOUNTER

The next morning Michael awoke when something touched his cheek. Startled and with arms flying, he opened his eyes to discover it was the dog from the night before. Standing not four meters away was a tall, heavyset man with a large hoe in his hands. Michael had heard nothing to alert him of their approach.

"Guten Morgen, junge Mann," said the tall man.
"Guten Morgen, mein Herr," Michael replied softly.

The tall man introduced himself as Herr Schnell, the farmer from the house on the distant hillside. Michael introduced himself simply as "Michael" without offering a last name.

"Are you hungry?" asked Herr Schnell.
"Wirklich viel" (very much), Michael replied.

The farmer reached into the large pouch hanging from his shoulder and pulled out a loaf of rye bread, a chunk of hard cheese, sausage, and some cold dumplings. Michael's face came alive with delight.

While Michael ate, Herr Schnell told him what to expect farther down the river. Rapids, then calm waters as he left the Harmersbach and entered the Kinzig, a much larger river that flowed into the Rhine near the town of Kehl.

"The upper reaches of the Kinzig can cause serious floods this time of year," Herr Schnell warned Michael. "Also, loggers in the nearby forests float large trees and large quantities of logs downriver to Kehl at this time of year, so be on the alert for log jams. Salmon will be spawning on the river, so you should have good luck fishing. Do you have any fishing line or hooks?"

When Michael shook his head "no," the tall man reached into his bag and produced some fishing line and hooks along with some bait. Michael could not believe his good fortune for having met this generous man.

Herr Schnell did not question Michael about where he had come from or why he was traveling down the river. However, he did volunteer some information to Michael.

He told him that he would see a number of old Roman castles downriver and advised Michael to be cautious of the second one he came to because the area was covered with tight-knit military fortifications that monitored the traffic on the river.

When Michael was finished eating, Herr Schnell produced the last of his gifts to Michael: a roughly hewn paddle that would help him navigate the river. The tall man helped shove Michael's raft to the river's edge and placed the remains of his shoulder bag onto the raft. After Michael got on board, Herr Schnell pushed the raft toward the current of the river, and with a wave of his hand and a pat on the head of his dog, he wished Michael, "Auf Wiedersehen und guten Ausflug!" He had nearly disappeared before Michael could return the wave.

As Michael paddled toward the swift moving water near the center of the river, he quickly realized the paddle that Herr Schnell gave him would make his journey much easier.

He soon approached the rapids and viewed the calmer water of the larger river Kinzig just around the final bend of the much smaller Harmersbach River. As he shifted his weight when the raft was lifted by the first rapid, he lost his balance and accidentally kicked the paddle into the rushing waters as he tried to right himself. He sat down and hung on for dear life as the raft bounced and heaved through what seemed like an eternity. Finally, things became somewhat calmer as his raft shot into the larger river.

This river was much calmer and the rocky banks were now replaced with gentle grass and flower-covered knolls. Michael sat back and let the current take him wherever it cared to as he enjoyed the beautiful new scenery.

The first castle appeared as he rounded a long sweeping bend in the river. Michael was much impressed with the size and beauty of the castle with its high turrets. He had never seen anything quite as massive, with its protective high walls. He marveled at the age of the structure and wondered how long it had taken the Romans to build it.

The next castle would be the one with military encampments that Herr Schnell had warned him of. He didn't have long to wait. As the sun reached what Michael thought to be late afternoon, he viewed an even larger castle in the mist on a far hill. At the rate he was now floating, he would be there in a few hours, or close to dusk. He thought hard about the military presence that would surely be there and what action he would have to take for his own safety.

CHAPTER 6
QUICK THOUGHTS AND QUICK ACTIONS!

As dusk approached, so did the mist. Michael felt somewhat exuberant that the growing density of the fog would shield him from view.

He lay flat on the small raft to help it pass undetected by the military, which he could now observe on the banks of the river. He thought about his recent brushes with the military, which caused him to leave home. He had previously been successful in eluding them and had every intention of doing the same this time. But now was different. There were no forests in which to become lost. This gave him pause and the fear of the unknown knotted and writhed in his empty stomach.

With each breath he drew closer to the military on the banks. The darkness of the growing evening surely would help mask his being discovered. His thoughts quickly changed when he observed rope netting across the river from bank to bank. Obviously this had been placed there to stop undetected passage on the river and to make sure a fee for passage was collected.

His body rigid and his fists clenched, Michael became numb with fear. A thunderbolt jagged him back to his senses just as the rope netting appeared before him and was about to snare his raft. With a quick leap he pushed himself off the raft and dove over the top of the rope netting. He felt the sudden chill of the river as its swift current closed over his head with an angry roar.

He held his breath for what seemed an eternity as he floated silently down the river. Rising to the surface, he took a quick breath and was astonished that he had been successful in escaping entrapment. The feeling of joy that was rising within him was short-lived. Although he enjoyed danger and excitement, he was now floating down the river without a raft. All of his personal belongings went overboard when the raft hit the netting. Everything he had was lost. How long could he stay afloat in this cool and dark water, and where would the water take him?

The river ran straight and deep for some time with Michael

floating on his back. His strength was beginning to ebb, and he knew he must get to the bank to rest and consider what he needed to do next for his continued survival.

With his strength waning, he swam across the currents of the river to the bank. The bank, however, was too high for him to climb out of the river. He had no choice but to float along the high bank until he came to an area where he could climb out. The river took a gentle bend and the current slowed. Finally, Michael's feet touched ground and he pushed himself into a small depression in the high bank. His eyes were full of sand and his bones ached as he sat down on the dry ground and breathed a sigh of relief.

The night was mellow and the tall grass of the bank comforting as he curled his exhausted body into a ball and quickly dropped off to sleep.

CHAPTER 7
THE SMELL OF FOOD

Michael awoke to the smell of eggs, sausage, and gruel cooking over a wood fire. He rolled over in the tall grass to let the rays of the sun feast on his face. Cautiously, he raised his head slightly above the tall grass to look in the direction of a man working with tools and singing. An excited voice, lifted to a shout, stopped everything dead. Michael quickly ducked back into the tall grass thinking he had been seen.

What seemed like an eternity passed as he lay there motionless. Softer voices drifted his way and he knew he had not been seen. He listened with increased intensity and detected a thick, clotty voice with an uneducated accent.

He crawled closer for a better look. There was a camp in the small clearing beyond which was a large pile of timber that had been recently cut from the nearby forest. Two young boys, about Michael's age, he assumed, were sitting on the ground around the morning fire with plates of food in their laps. A muscular, big, and bad-tempered man stood on the other side of the fire, demanding that the young boys hurry and finish their breakfast.

As Michael's mouth watered from the smell of breakfast, he decided it would be safe to approach the small gathering and request a share. With his stomach growling, he rose and walked slowly toward the group. They all turned to observe Michael's arrival but gave no sign of trepidation. It was obvious this stranger had been invited by the smell of their food.

The muscular older man's voice softened with a greeting to Michael to come join them. With a "vielen Dank," Michael moved quickly before the offer could be withdrawn. The two boys greeted him with some curiosity but gave him a plate and served him a few spoonfuls of gruel and a piece of sausage. While Michael was consuming this, the boys placed a large salmon over the flames.

The older man eyed Michael's young muscular body and knew in an instant that he was a farm boy accustomed to hard work. He explained to Michael who they were and what they did for a living way out here near the forest and river's edge. The three of them were timber rafters preparing to take the fallen logs downriver to a larger operation at Mannheim. The man then asked Michael if he would join them because one of their crew had recently been injured and they needed someone to replace him. He told Michael he would be paid the same wages as the fourth man, who was now recuperating from his injuries.

Michael could not believe his luck and was quick to accept. It was a short time later, when the job was explained in more detail, that Michael grew a bit concerned and felt caught in a web of his own making. The job entailed tying three or four logs together tightly, then riding and steering them, with large rudders, down the main course of the river to Mannheim. Michael learned that the job wasn't much different than his previous days' rafting trip. The only difference was the size of the raft and the addition of a rudder.

It was not until the other boys had their logs in the water that Michael learned it was on one of their previous trips downriver that the original fourth man was severely injured. His raft came apart and he was thrown into the raging water between the bouncing logs. His head was severely cracked open, and he was rescued only moments before he lost consciousness. The fact that the man had not tied his logs together securely had been deemed the cause of the accident. Michael worked feverishly to make sure he would not meet a similar fate.

CHAPTER 8
A TRUE BALANCING ACT

The older man told Michael to watch the other young men carefully, as they shoved off from the riverbanks. They stood erect on the three or four logs that each joined the large rudder at the rear in a kind of cradle. They pushed and pulled this large rudder back and forth, guiding the logs toward the center of the river. With each push or pull they were careful not to step off of the security of the logs underfoot. Things looked simple enough to Michael as he assured the older man he understood.

Michael was now ready to push off on his new adventure riding the logs downriver. His balance was good, and being a fast learner, he had his logs in the main current immediately. The older man stood on the riverbank watching appreciatively and gave Michael a wave of support.

They did not stop for lunch but kept going until early

evening, when they stopped at an easily accessed cove on the river. It was a very welcome break after a long, stressful day. Michael considered that the day had just taken him farther from all the problems he had left behind. Other than having tired muscles, he felt fine, even invigorated. With two good meals under his belt and a solid night's sleep, he was the first to be ready and eager to move on down the river. The older man grinned with approval.

When the faster current in the center of the river caught the logs, only a little rudder control was necessary. This gave Michael time to observe the scenery passing before him.

The black forest that he had known as a boy was now behind him, replaced by gentle rolling hills covered with heavy grass as far as he could see. Occasionally a small castle would appear and disappear as the current carrying the logs rounded a bend in the river. As they passed various small villages, people standing on the riverbanks waved their encouragement.

The days came and went, and life was almost monotonous as the three boys and the man approached their destination of Kehl on the Rhine. Some questions from the other two boys stirred Michael's thoughts, and he promised himself to be more circumspect with the answers he gave them.

His caution proved important, as they finally reached Kehl. Michael observed one of the two boys disappearing rather quickly after positioning his logs in the alcove where hundreds of other logs were being stored. Michael watched him move stealthily toward the larger buildings in the main section of the town. His attention was diverted by loud shouting next to the water.

The logs from their rafts were being pulled from the water by horses, block and tackles, and sheer brute strength and placed on higher ground where the logs would lay drying for a number of months or even a year depending on their size. Michael observed hundreds, perhaps thousands, of logs stacked neatly on the gentle sloping hillsides to dry. Michael learned that as the logs dried they were combined into larger rafts that would be taken down the Rhine River to Mannheim and from there to their final destination, Rotterdam in the Netherlands. Michael made up his mind, then and there, to seek a job rafting the logs all the way.

Michael had found the perfect escape route, especially

when he discovered that Rotterdam was an ocean harbor where large ships docked to pick up loads of various goods, passengers, and supplies for long voyages to various lands. The grandness of his ambitions kept his mind whirling. But what about the boy, whom he thought of as his friend, who was now hurrying toward the main section of town? Michael's face tightened as he searched for possible reasons for his friend's actions.

CHAPTER 9
A MAJOR MISCALCULATION

Michael put his ominous thoughts in the back of his mind as he approached the main gathering of loggers around the fire pit preparing dinner. He was greeted amicably by the older men and soon learned that age had little if any effect on his acceptance into this hardy, muscular group. Sharing the same dangers of the river and the logs themselves knit a kindred relationship such that Michael had not previously encountered in his young life. The feelings he now enjoyed, along with this new experience, made him feel safe and contented.

He pitched in to help prepare dinner and then sat down on a nearby log to eat his first meal since breakfast. He looked up from his tin plate to see the boy he had previously observed rushing into town. Only now, the boy was hurriedly approaching the group with two official-looking men walking beside him.

Michael dropped his tin plate and somersaulted backward over the log he had been sitting on in a clumsy attempt to hide himself from view. As the tin plate hit the ground with a clatter and a clang, the older loggers seated nearby took heed of Michael's action with wonder and concern.

Two of the older loggers moved quickly down the log to where Michael had been seated to further hide him. Had they moved quickly enough, or had such movements betrayed them and called particular attention to them? Only time would tell. The loggers fell silent as the threesome approached their clustered group.

The silence was short-lived as the loggers recognized their employer, Herr Groetsch, his older son Rolf, and younger son Helmut. After extending greetings all around, Herr Groetsch surveying the gathered group, asking where Michael was. "I want to meet him," he said.

Michael peered out from his protected hiding place. His face tightened and his adrenaline level began to rise at the sound of the commanding voice of Herr Groetsch. After a few more moments of silence and with the general sounds and comments of the other gathered loggers, Michael's fear dissipated. With a quick intake of breath like someone about to plunge into icy water, he rose and said, "I am Michael, the one you seek."

Seeing Michael emerge from his hiding place, Herr Groetsch smiled at him and motioned to him to come closer. Michael's tension rose with each faltering step forward. His heart thumping against his rib cage, his body rigid and fists clenched, he slowly approached Herr Groetsch.

Herr Groetsch, noting Michael's fear, quickly assured the boy that nothing harmful was about to be bestowed on him. He wished merely to compliment Michael for his quick grasp of logging and was eager to meet the young man of whom Helmut raved.

A permanent job was offered to Michael in hopes he would continue his journey downriver. Michael's face beamed with pleasure as he quickly accepted before another word could be spoken.

After dinner and further celebrations, Michael fell reluctantly but happily into a deep sleep.

CHAPTER 10
DOWNRIVER TO ROTTERDAM

Up early the next morning and anxious to get going, the feeling of happiness rising inside him, Michael felt relaxed and invincible.

The bundling of large dried logs was completed quickly, and Michael was assigned the third pilot to leave. He had only to follow the more experienced loggers ahead of him.

He found it easy to mimic the more experienced loggers as they guided their huge logs around each new bend in the Rhine River and through the occasional narrowing, faster waters.

All loggers delivered their logs safely to their final destination of Rotterdam without any major incidents along the way. Michael was amazed when he received money in hand for his efforts and an offer to return upriver to continue his relationship with Herr Groetsch's logging company.

Michael thanked all his new friends and reluctantly told them he wished to continue his journey to America. Some had heard little about America and quizzed him further. After hearing Michael's tales, which he had learned from his teacher, many expressed sadness that they could not join him on his exciting adventure.

As Michael finally parted, he was wished "gut Glück" and "auf Wiedersehen." He walked briskly toward the docks of the large ships in the Rotterdam harbor. He hoped to gain passage to America as quickly as possible.

This feat was not as easy as he had hoped. Although he heard much of his native language being spoken, the new language he was now encountering was similar but yet impossible to understand. He recognized immediately he needed someone to help him.

Luckily a lad about his same age recognized his quandary and quickly came to his aid. Hans had arrived a number of months before and had learned this new language well enough to communicate sufficiently. The two of them struck up a friendship.

Through Hans, who worked for the Netherlands Steamship Company, Michael was introduced to the captain of the recently built *Rotterdam Westphalia.* The maiden voyage would be to Philadelphia in America, and both Hans and Michael obtained jobs working on the ship.

The *Rotterdam Westphalia* was the latest in steamship technology. Ocean-going steamships had been gathering popularity in recent years. She was a very heavy ship with four durable wooden hulls and was designed to compete with the ships built by the Cunard Steamship Company of Great Britain, a company that had a virtual monopoly on the North Atlantic. Like the Cunard ships, no provisions were made for steerage passengers. Speedy and safe delivery of mail was the goal rather than shipboard comforts.

Michael was invited to further inspect this fabulous new ship. He discovered to his amazement that it wasn't a pure steamship at all, but rather a sailing ship with steam engines and a great side paddle wheel. He was told that the sails are used whenever possible, both to enhance speed and to promote fuel economy, since coal was bulky and expensive.

Under the best conditions, the ship should be capable of reaching America in about 10 days, not counting delays for refueling or the necessary scraping of salt deposits from her boiler. This was a very dirty and time-consuming job that required stopping the ship's engines every few days for 24 hours.

At the conclusion of the ship's tour, Michael learned his main responsibility would be to stoke the boilers with coal and scrape away the accumulated salt deposits. In addition, he was to care for the occasional needs of the few paying passengers that may be aboard. This sounded quite acceptable to him as he thought back on his recent dangerous trip down the Rhine on the log floats. Little did he know what was in store for him.

CHAPTER 11
OFF TO AMERICA

Within the week, the *Rotterdam Westphalia* was prepared for its maiden voyage to America. Michael was eager to leave and had all the necessary provisions for the journey that his meager income would permit.

The full crew had assembled for the captain's instructions of what he expected of his crew and other details surrounding the actual voyage. He mentioned that there would be twelve paying passengers aboard in the five small cabins on the *Westphalia*. The captain pointed out that the passengers were secondary to the delivery of the mail and the various goods in the cargo hold. He expected the crew to treat the passengers cordially but not let them interfere with the crew's primary duties.

They set out to sea the next morning to catch the outgoing tide. Many of the ship construction workers were on the dock to provide a joyous send-off. Michael stood at the ship's railing excitingly waving his good-bye to the continent he was leaving rather than to the crowd that had gathered to see the ship off.

As the tide caught the ship and moved it into the main channel, Michael promptly returned to the boiler room to begin his arduous duty of stoking the fire in the boilers. He quickly found this duty to be both monotonous and tiring.

For the first few days Michael worked long hours, both during the day and at night. The ship performed as intended but was using more fuel than anticipated as it sailed southward down the English Channel.

Michael soon learned that not all passengers had boarded in Rotterdam and that the ship would be stopping near Portsmouth, England not only to welcome the rest of the passengers aboard but also to replenish fuel for their trip across the Atlantic. Fuel was less expensive in England than it was in the Netherlands, so the stop pleased Michael and his sense of frugality.

While the ship was replenishing fuel, Michael and his friend Hans explored Portsmouth. Both were intrigued by the differences in dress, customs, language, and food. They found a hearty handshake, a shrug, a quick smile, or a wave of "Hello" went a long way in communicating in this strange new country.

The new passengers arrived mid-morning of the second day in port. Michael stood at the railing to observe their boarding and was curious about an attractive young girl, about his own age, accompanied by whom he assumed was her mother and father. Michael thought, "This trip may be more interesting than I had hoped!"

CHAPTER 12
THE CROSSING

The paddle wheel was doing its job, and Michael and Hans appeared to be doing their jobs. The *Rotterdam Westphalia* was performing exactly as intended. Unexpectantly, on the third day out of Portsmouth, the paddle wheels began slowing and soon came to a complete stop. Quickly, the sails were set and the ship was again navigable.

Michael and Hans discovered what the inside of the boiler looked like. The boiler was permitted to cool before the two could enter to begin scraping and chipping the various deposits that had gathered on the sides and valves from the salty seawater. This was a difficult, hot, stinky job that had to be done. However, it occurred much sooner than anticipated, which indicated some filtering problems existed somewhere in the incoming water line. This would take the engineer's time to correct, thus slowing down their crossing time. The ship had to continue under sail power until the redesign was completed.

Michael appreciated the break in his duties and spent much time on deck soaking up the fresh air and the sunshine. It was during this time that he became acquainted with Jenny, the young girl who had come aboard in Portsmouth. With their waves and their smiles, their communication seemed almost complete. Language was the final barrier to be broken.

They spent much time together. Michael learned her parents were of German descent and that she spoke a little German. The family was returning to their home in Pittsburg, Pennsylvania after completing a business trip to the continent.

Michael began learning basic English, which he knew he would need in the United States of America. Jenny was his teacher as they sat and laughed together, rocking with the motion of the ship. Their friendship deepened with each hour and day so spent.

On more than one occasion, Jenny's father joined in for a lively discussion on various subjects. The group used a mixture of German and English, as the situation demanded. Some of the crew members found this amusing, but their laughter did not interfere with the bilingual conversations. The group talked about business, life in general, what to expect in America, and the importance of choice and of freedom itself. Many times after such discussions, Michael's mind would spin and thoughts would wash over him like the waves, at times, washed over the bow of the ship.

After the boiler's filtering system was fixed, Michael's time with Jenny became less frequent. Tending the boiler fire assumed its original position in his daily activities, and the paddle wheel returned to its full capability.

Even though time together was much more limited now, Michael and Jenny still found time to permit their friendship to grow. One day out from landing at the port in Philadelphia, Jenny gave Michael her father's business card. On the reverse side she had written her home address in Pittsburg and the short message: "Friends forever." This was their last time alone together, and they departed with a smile and a wave.

CHAPTER 13
ARRIVAL IN PHILADELPHIA

Excitement on board grew as America came into view. As the ship drew toward shore docking, Michael stood on deck gazing at the wondrous buildings of Philadelphia. He welcomed the sights and sounds of this new world and new adventure. This city, he learned, was the "birth place" of the country he was about to enter. Michael learned from one of the ship guests that the original thirteen colonies of 1776 had doubled in size to twenty-six states, which now formed the United States of America.

Michael's first step off the ship onto the ground of his newly chosen country was most daunting yet exciting to his every sense.

Michael stood alone to one side, a bit bewildered, as those who had been passengers disappeared into the crowd that had gathered to celebrate the conclusion of the *Rotterdam Westphalia*'s maiden voyage. He shook off his sad feelings as he caught his last glimpse of Jenny, who had turned to wave a final "good-bye" to him.

With ever growing bewilderment, Michael stood wondering where to go and what to do. Leaning against a post, he reached into his knapsack and pulled out a pamphlet his teacher had given him. This pamphlet had been widely distributed by the Giessen Emigration Society in southwestern Germany. It urged readers to join the society and help found a free German state in North America. The Giessener Gesellschaft Society had developed plans to concentrate Germans in a territory that could eventually be admitted to the Union as a German state. Missouri, Texas, and Wisconsin were three states that came under consideration. The headquarters of the Giessener Gesellschaft Society was in Germantown, Philadelphia.

Not far from where he was standing, a group of German speakers were welcoming a small group of Germans whom Michael had seen on board the *Rotterdam Westphalia*. A good place to start, Michael thought. He approached the group with hat in hand. The circle opened to admit him with a "guten Tag." It was quite obvious who the Americans were by their dress and cleanliness. Michael asked if anyone in the group knew where or how he could contact someone in the Giessener Gesellschaft Society. Bright smiles broke out among the group along with a few chuckles as they announced, “You already have made that contact. We are they.”

CHAPTER 14
LIFE IN GERMANTOWN, PHILADELPHIA

With his eyebrows rising in obvious pleasure, Frimut Buhl came forward to greet the newcomer. Michael's lips lifted in a tight smile. Herr Buhl's appearance was typically German, causing Michael to remember and miss his family and friends back home. As they greeted each other, this picture of home was lost and no longer in focus. Michael licked his lower lip and shared his hopes and dreams with Herr Buhl.

He hoped to find a paying job to provide the necessities of life and to supplement the little money he had been able to save during his journey. The two talked for some time about his singular journey and about Michael's education, experiences, and rationale for leaving everything behind in search of a better, freer life.

During their discussions, Michael learned immigration into the United States was subject to virtually no legal restrictions. Essentially anyone who wanted to enter the United States could do so. Foreigners simply got off the ship and went about their business. However, there was opposition among some U.S. citizens that such rules could cause wages to fall, especially for unskilled workers. Others in the group willingly provided their own interesting stories.

Roeder Kleberga, a heavyset man with dark blue eyes and a trim mustache, stood out in the group and Michael felt he was being appraised for some unknown reason. Kleberga approached Michael during a break in the conversation and pulled him aside.

Herr Kleberga paused for a moment, as if hesitant to speak his mind. “I hear you have some experience with butchering,” he said finally, “and I would like to offer you a job in my butcher shop.”

Whereas this was somewhat true, Michael’s experience was limited to butchering a goat, a deer, and a great number of chickens. However, Michael did not correct Kleberga’s assumptions and instead committed himself to learn quickly anything he did not already know.

Michael spent the next several months doing whatever Kleberga assigned him to do. The days were long and repetitious, but Michael made no complaints. Although he wished for his own room, away from the butcher shop and its odors of blood and death, he was grateful to Herr Kleberga for permitting him to sleep in a small room at the back of the shop while he got himself situated.

With what little time off that he could find, he attended schooling provided by the Giessener Gesellschaft Society. This schooling covered American history and the English language, both of which Michael knew were essential to his new life.

The months passed slowly and devoid of any adventure. But Michael sensed that things would soon change.

CHAPTER 15
THE AWAKENING

Yes! Michael thought. His arrival in America had been fulfilled. He had found true freedom: freedom of thought and freedom of purpose. He had learned the English language enough to get by in any discussion or situation, and he had some extra money saved. Now, he surmised, was the right time for more adventure.

He fondly recalled Jenny, from his boat trip crossing the Atlantic, and remembered she had suggested after he got settled, that she would like to know what he thought of this new world. The railroad line to Pittsburg had recently been completed and he yearned for an exploratory trip there, not only to see Jenny but to travel on a train for the first time. Being a man of action, before the day was over, he had purchased a train ticket for his next day off work.

When he arrived in Pittsburg, he sought directions to Jenny's home, which he discovered was but a short distance from the train station. As he walked, he observed what life was like in Pittsburg.

Passing through a vegetable farmers market, he observed a young lady with a basket obviously picking up items for her family or for the house where she worked. He thought it was probably the latter, since she was rather shabbily dressed. He followed her through the market, observing her every movement.

He was rather taken with this peasant girl and decided to approach her. He noted she was about to purchase some meat. "Excuse me, Miss," he said politely, "but that piece of meat would not be the best choice."

He could see that the young woman was taken back by such a bold move and unwelcomed statement, so he added, "Please forgive me. I am a butcher's helper in Germantown. I suggest you take the tenderloin," he said pointing. "With its marbling, it will be more flavorful and tender."

"Thank you," the young lady said, recovering her composure. She asked if this was his first visit to Pittsburg, and they proceeded through the market selecting various vegetables and fruits to accompany the tenderloin. She introduced herself as Philomene and told him that she worked as a domestic servant cooking and cleaning for a well-to-do family. She told him she had been working there for a number of years and had to get back to the house to help prepare dinner.

Philomene smiled and thanked Michael for his help. As an afterthought, she suggested that should he find himself in Pittsburg at another time to please seek her out either at her place of work or at the market. She said since she frequently made trips to the market she would most likely be found there. She seemed reluctant for him to visit her at the home where she worked. Michael left the market with a smile on his face and a renewed interest in visiting Pittsburg again.

He proceeded to Jenny's home, the girl he had met on the ocean crossing and with whom he originally intended to visit. On approaching the home, he saw it was a mansion and not a simple house. As he walked up the path to the front door, he was taken with the apparent value of the property, the farm animals, and the crops surrounding the area.

Somewhat reluctantly he knocked on the door and was greeted by a servant. He explained that he was there to see Jenny. The servant invited him in and directed him to wait in the drawing room. While awaiting her arrival, he looked around the room, truly impressed with the elegance of his surroundings. Never before had he been exposed to such riches. He felt somewhat uncomfortable and out of place.

These feelings quickly vanished when he saw Jenny tripping lightly down the stairs with a huge smile on her face. She took Michael by the hand and led him to the veranda. They sipped glasses of lemonade with a sprig of mint and reminisced about the trip from England and what had happened since then. They talked just as old friends would normally talk and she asked his impressions about his new life in the United States.

After a couple of hours of visiting over a light lunch, she mentioned that she was obliged to prepare for a function her family was attending that evening. So as the afternoon began to wane, Michael excused himself, thanked her courteously for the visit, and walked back to the train station.

On the train back to Philadelphia, he promised himself that he would return to Pittsburg on his next day off, not to see Jenny but rather to find Philomene and to further their acquaintance.

Michael returned to the butcher shop and resumed what had now become a rather boring job. He felt he had learned enough English and ways of this new country to step out on his own without the help of the German fraternity that had been so kind to him up until now.

CHAPTER 16
RECALLING "TAKE YOUR STAND, MAKE YOUR MARK"

On one trip to the center of Philadelphia, Michael saw a great deal of activity surrounding a group waving flags and holding signs. The signs read such things as "Mexico, don't tread on us" and "Down with Mexico." People were hurrying around, shouting, and men were stepping up to a table to sign their names on a sheet of paper. On the other side of the table was a uniformed soldier. Seeing the soldier caused a sudden shiver up Michael's spine because of his experiences as he left Germany.

As one of the young men who had just signed his name walked past Michael, he said, "You're next!"

Michael asked, "For what?" It was then that Michael learned that the United States had declared war on Mexico. Michael wondered about the reason behind such action. He stepped up to the table to inquire.

He was told much more, by the people around the table, than his mind could absorb in this brief encounter. He knew that Frimut Buhl of the Giessener Gesellschaft Society, who had been a big help in his life, up until now, would be able to correctly and fully inform him about what he had just heard. He promised himself to contact Herr Buhl as soon as possible.

Michael continued his visits to various areas of Philadelphia unconcerned with this latest news. However, as Michael heard more about the war, he knew it was time to visit with Herr Buhl.

He found Herr Buhl well-informed on the latest news of the war and they spent thc next couple of hours in discussion.

Michael learned that when Mexico won its independence from Spain in 1821, the territory it possessed included Mexico, most of Central America, and the western territories of California, Nevada, Utah, Texas, and as well as parts of Colorado, Arizona, New Mexico, and Wyoming. In 1835 Mexican President Antonio López de Santa Anna took measures to transform Mexico from a federal republic to a centralist republic. This move prompted Central

America and Texas to secede from Mexico. Texas defeated Santa Anna and his armies and became a separate republic in 1836. Mexico saw Texas as a rebellious province to be reincorporated at a later date – preferably by diplomatic means, but by force if necessary. The Mexican government warned the United States that annexation would mean war.

Michael further learned that former U.S. president John Tyler and the current president, James Polk, wished to extend U.S. territories to the Pacific Coast, fulfilling the "Manifest Destiny" of the country. The U.S. government offered to purchase the lands, but the Mexican government refused to negotiate. Texas was admitted to the United States in December 1845. Shortly thereafter, U.S. patrols were attacked along the Rio Grande River, and the United States declared war on Mexico on May 13, 1846.

Having learned the reasons why America declared war on Mexico, Michael became more interested in discovering what requirements were involved in serving in the U.S. Army, what the pay would be, and what it would be like in the service. He thought about all of these things as he continued his tedious work in the butcher shop.

CHAPTER 17
SEEKING NEW ADVENTURES

Weighing his future at the butcher shop, Michael sought to improve his life with new adventures. Philadelphia had become almost unbearable. German and Irish immigrants had swelled the population of the city and its suburbs, including Germantown. Michael was aware of the tenements, boarding houses, row houses, and small streets and the filth and garbage that accompanied this now overcrowded area. The smell of manure from animal pens could not go unnoticed, and hundreds of people were dying each year from diseases such as smallpox, malaria, tuberculosis, and cholera. It was time to leave!

Michael said his good-byes and enlisted in the army on April 25, 1846. Immediately, there arose the question whether he had enlisted in the regular U.S. Army or in the Pennsylvania Volunteer Regiment. The difference was to become important later.

The majority of those enlisting were in their late teens and early twenties. Most had never been away from home. They enlisted, in most cases, in search of glory and adventure. What they got, more often than not, was a bitter dose of reality: heat, dust, boredom, insects, disease, and, all too frequently, death – more often caused by illness than by enemy bullets.

Michael was astonished when he received his clothing rations. Never in his life had he possessed such an abundance of clothing. The items he received were the following:

1 Dress cap
2 Pairs drawers
1 Woolen jacket
1 Cotton jacket
1 Leather or silk shako
3 Pairs woolen overalls
1 Pair boots
1 Blanket

2 Flannel shirts
1 Uniform coat
1 Fatigue frock

1 Tall shako
1 Pair cotton overalls
3 Pairs stockings
1 Muzzle-loading musket

Volunteers wore a variety of uniforms, often modeled after the uniforms of the regular army. Michael's regiment was issued tall shakos, but these were soon abandoned in favor of lighter forage caps. The muzzle-loading muskets had been selected because they were quicker and easier to load, although their range and accuracy left something to be desired.

He learned that his pay scale was going to be $8 per month rather than the $6 he had been told when he enlisted. This higher amount had been offered by the officials because additional men were required and enlistments had been slower than anticipated. Michael was overjoyed with his good fortune.

It was not long before Michael learned that the regiment was not paid on a regular basis. This was a sore point with the men and a major source of dissatisfaction and low morale. They were promised that their money would accrue and be paid at a later date.

Army life soon became a drag for most volunteers. Up early for drilling, firearm practice, and learning to obey all orders became painfully routine. Little did Michael know that this routine would be considerably altered within the month.

CHAPTER 18
THE LONG ROAD TO BATTLE

Michael's recruit training in Carlisle, Pennsylvania was short and tenuous. Colonel E. V. Sumner had recently been appointed commander of the Pennsylvania Volunteer Regiment. Colonel Sumner called the regiment to general assembly to inform them that they would be leaving within a few days to join the "Army of the West" at Fort Leonard Wood, Missouri, commanded by General Zachary Taylor and to prepare themselves accordingly.

Travel to Fort Leonard Wood was by no means easy, but Michael found it both invigorating and interesting. They were sent by rail to Harrisburg, Pennsylvania and then by canal to a point well within the Allegheny Mountains, over the mountains on foot, by canal to Pittsburg, Pennsylvania, then down the Ohio and Mississippi rivers by steamboat and up the Missouri River to Fort Leavenworth. Michael viewed this as a true adventure.

During their stay at Fort Leonard Wood, the soldiers considered themselves very comfortable sleeping on bed sacks filled once a month with what they called "prairie feathers." In addition, each had a pair of soldier blankets and an overcoat that did double-duty as a pillow.

Meals, however, were a different matter. The food was abominable. Often, when they broke a biscuit, they could see it move, if the critters had not already died from cating the bad flour. The pork and bacon were of the same character. If not for the wild beef that they regularly shot, they would starve.

A day didn't pass that the regiment did not learn of new deaths among its numbers. These deaths were due mainly to unsanitary camp conditions, which resulted from the ignorance of men who had no idea how disease was spread. Michael longed to be gone from this place.

Shortly, Michael learned that Colonel Stephen Kearny would lead the Army of the West into New Mexico and occupy the territory for the United States. The march was to take them by Bent's Fort in Colorado Territory, through Cimarron Canyon in northern New Mexico, and on into

Santa Fe. The 6,000 soldiers, 250 wagons, and 2,000 oxen, mules, and horses covered the 900 miles to Santa Fe in 50 days but not without the army suffering en route.

The wagons accompanying the army were poorly distributed. Tents and utensils were not always with the proper company. One instance of intense hunger within Michael's company caused volunteers within the company to attack a wagon and appropriate the contents despite the objections of the driver, who said it was a "through" wagon and was not to be opened until arrival in Santa Fe. Officers looked the other way and equally enjoyed the bounty.

On reaching Santa Fe, General Zachary Taylor reorganized the army, which had grown, with new arrivals, to more than 15,000 troops. A portion was to proceed to California and occupy that area. The second portion was to travel to Monterey, Mexico and capture that city.

The Pennsylvania Volunteer Regiment, which Michael belonged to, remained with Taylor's army and on September 19, the regiment, along with approximately 6,000 soldiers, arrived on the outskirts of Monterey, facing the Mexican Army estimated at 5,000 men. The battle began the next morning. Michael's regiment marched into battle with their guns blazing. They returned fire to the withering fire being received from the enemy's muskets and cannons thundering at them from the fortified hilltop.

The evening of the first day's battle, Michael's squad discussed their feelings and the raw courage they had had to summon to charge the enemy knowing they were putting their lives in danger. The battle lasted 4 long days and cost the lives of 450 U.S. soldiers and an equal number of Mexican soldiers.

Following the Mexican request for a parley, the two sides agreed on an 8-week armistice and the Mexican forces, unrepentantly, marched away with their weapons on September 25, giving the city over to the Americans. It was reported throughout the ranks that President James Polk was furious over these terms and subsequently plotted the end of Taylor's career.

Michael found his first taste of battle frightening, but it matched what he had been told during his recruitment training. Captain Scott complimented him for his firing accuracy. Michael had become well acquainted with his musket and had learned to compensate for its built-in inaccuracies.

As is typical with all armies, there was a regrouping and a period of time before the next battle. During this time the army continued vigorous training and discipline to keep their men occupied while more supplies arrived that would be needed for the next action.

The waiting weighed on all of the soldiers, and they found it most difficult to endure this “hurry up and wait” attitude of their officers.

During these 4 or 5 months of winter, they survived by telling stories, playing card games, and gambling. Michael found the gambling not to his liking, partly because he had not been paid actual cash since he joined the regiment. Boredom set in.

CHAPTER 19
THE BATTLE OF CERRO GORDO

In early spring 1847, news reached Zachary Taylor's army of the successes the U.S. Army had had in other areas. One particular piece of news that intrigued Michael and his fellow buddies was that the United States was opening a second front against Mexico. There was to be an amphibious landing near Veracruz. After taking this city, the U.S. troops, under General Winfield Scott, were to march on to Mexico City in hopes of ending the war swiftly.

A vanguard of scouts now informed General Zachary Taylor that the Mexican general, Antonio López de Santa Anna, had regrouped after his defeat at Buena Vista and marched his 12,000 determined Mexican soldiers toward the coast and the invading Americans. They were now dug in and well fortified at Cerro Gordo, or "Fat Hill," near Xalapa. It was a good defensive position. But Santa Anna foolishly ignored reports that his left flank was vulnerable. He thought the ravines and dense chaparral to his left made it impossible for the Americans to attack from there.

General Scott exploited this weakness and ordered Captain Robert E. Lee to attack from a trail hastily cut through the brush that would avoid Santa Anna's artillery. This path of attack was used by 7,000 men while 3,000 men attacked the Mexican front. This plan cut off the Mexicans' line of retreat and captured their camps. The battle was a rout. An estimated 1,000 Mexican soldiers were killed or wounded and another 3,000 captured along with their artillery and supplies. U.S. losses were little more than 400.

Michael's squad captured Santa Anna during this battle and discovered he had a hoard of gold and silver coins stashed in the hollow of his wooden leg. The value was estimated to be $18,000. Santa Anna and his leather-colored wooden leg were turned over to regimental guards. In the confusion of the battle's aftermath, Santa Anna escaped by exchanging uniforms with a lowly private in his army and expediently mounting a nearby horse and riding to safety.

This battle put the Mexican Army in full retreat and disarray to Mexico City. In the summer and early fall, a number of other battles were fought and in each case the battles were decisively won by the U.S. forces.

Now most of Mexico was in the hands of the U.S. military with the exception of a fortress at the top of Chapultepec Hill. The fortress was also Mexico's military academy and many of the young cadets fought in its defense.

After a day of pounding Chapultepec with cannons and mortars, General Scott sent parties with scaling ladders to storm the fortress. Once the fortress fell, the city gates were not far behind. By nightfall General Santa Anna had decided to abandon the city with the few soldiers he had left. Mexico City belonged to the invaders, and Mexican authorities were ready to negotiate. The Treaty of Guadalupe Hidalgo was approved in May 1848 by both governments, with Mexico ceding vast Mexican territories to the United States.

Peace arrived at last, and Michael was more than ready to return to the life he had left.

CHAPTER 20
HOMEWARD BOUND

Michael's return to Philadelphia was uneventful and closely followed the reverse of the trip that took him into battle a few years previously. He wished to put the war behind him as quickly as possible. Happiness rose inside him as his thoughts turned again to the girl he had met at the farmers market, Philomene, who had hair the color of rich honey.

He had thought of her many times during various lulls in the war. Whereas others of his compatriots had received occasional letters from home or loved ones, he had received none. He felt there must be some reason since he had left word with her that would have permitted such contact if she so desired. There was an uneasiness in his heart as he recalled they had never been more than careful strangers to each other. He was determined to contact her as soon as possible after his return to Philadelphia.

Shortly after his return, the regiment was called to order and told to gather their personal items and all army equipment and proceed to the quartermaster's tent. There they were to turn in their firearms and other equipment, receive any pay due, and be mustered out.

Michael did as he was told but ran into a difficult situation as the paymaster was processing his discharge. Michael had not been paid, at any point, during his service, yet the paymaster had no record of his existence or that any payment was due. The paymaster acknowledged him as the "invisible soldier" and informed him there was nothing that he could do concerning either his payment or his discharge. The paymaster suggested that Michael speak with the adjutant general.

An argument with the paymaster ensued until a full colonel interceded and formally dismissed Michael with a wave of his hand. Michael's mind drifted into fuzzy haze as he breathed an exasperated sigh. He now realized that he was in for a touch of heavy-handed drama since military time was so sluggish that movement could scarcely be noted.

The days passed slowly as he awaited an appointment with

the adjutant general, but finally it came. Michael related the whole story of his enlistment, the battles in which he had fought, and the fact that he had not been paid the amount promised on his enlistment. The general and his aides all shook their heads knowingly.

The words of the adjutant general rang in Michael's ears. "I fear in your hurry to join the war effort, you did not attend to one very important matter." Michael braced himself for the next comment. "You probably enlisted in the regular U.S. Army rather than the Pennsylvania Volunteer Regiment." The general explained that men signing up for the volunteer regiments had their choice of 1 to 2 years or for the length of the war and that signing up for the U.S. Army would have been for a 5-year period. "You may have signed up for the U.S. Army but then been sent in error to the Pennsylvania Volunteer Regiment," the general said.

Nothing could contain Michael's strained nervousness. He took a deep breath and then plunged forward, telling the general that he was sorry to find him so great a stickler for minute military regulations. Michael's own officers, with whom he had served the past 2 years and fought in many battles, would vouch for him and the fact that he had been placed in keeping with his enlistment – that being with the Pennsylvania Volunteer Regiment.

Michael was told that his initial enlistment would be thoroughly investigated and straightened out. At that time, and only at that time, would he be paid and appropriately released from service. Nothing further could be done until the investigation was complete. The meeting with the adjutant general was over.

CHAPTER 21
BIDING HIS TIME

The regiment with whom he had served throughout the war was now mustered out. Michael was shuffled from one volunteer regiment to another as each was released from duty.

Time served with each of these regiments was short in duration. Michael found that he received his bedding and food requirements but escaped any ordered or assigned duties. He was recognized on their rosters but truly became the "invisible soldier" in both action and deed. He did pretty much as he desired and answered to no one.

Although this became a welcome change from his past army experiences, his whole life was in limbo. He had no money and could not leave the camp without a day or overnight pass.

He longed to follow his thoughts of the young girl he had met in the market years previously. He was determined to find a way.

One such temporary regiment to which he was assigned was a cavalry unit. The soldiers of this unit were anxious to leave their duties behind and wanted to be mustered out as quickly as possible. These cavalry soldiers took the attitude of shirking the duties that were normally required of them. Simple tasks such as cleaning the horse stalls on a regular basis and grooming the horses now became a chore for them.

Michael saw his opportunity to earn money. He approached a number of them and offered to clean the stalls and groom the horses while they enjoyed free time either in camp or on pass. These cavalry soldiers' monthly pay was $8 so the fees charged would have to be in line with this pay.

The price for such service was bargained and finally determined. For cleaning one horse stall, Michael would receive $.25, which was equal to about a day's pay for the soldier. He would receive a fee of $.50 for grooming the horse since that would take longer and was considered a more important job. The stalls would need to be cleaned twice a week and the horses groomed once during that period.

This meant that Michael would receive $1.50 every two weeks from the soldiers that enlisted his service. He quickly found his otherwise free days of the past were totally gone. He had as much business as he could handle and began making a nice income for as long as that particular outfit awaited their release. Every few weeks he had to start all over to rebuild business with the new cavalry units now returning. It was not difficult for him to be assigned to the units that he found the most lucrative.

His income problem was now handled and he had money in his pocket for the first time in years. Obtaining desirable passes outside of camp was his next goal. This he thought might take more ingenuity since most soldiers relished their time away from camp and the accompanying military duties. This was especially so for those waiting to be mustered out.

"Eureka!" he thought. In every army outfit, there were some who loved to gamble and would eventually lose all their money. Michael thought, why not take some of the monies from his lucrative business to purchase passes from these gamblers? He would be helping them with their gambling addiction by providing them the wherewithal to continue their gambling while helping the "invisible soldier" follow his dreams away from camp.

The cost for each pass had to be enough to make it attractive, yet not so much that soldiers would stampede to him, causing officers to notice. Michael decided to offer $.75 for a 1-day pass, $2 for a 2-day pass, and $3 for a 3-day pass.

Word quickly but quietly passed among the enlisted soldiers and Michael soon had sufficient contacts to satisfy his requirements. Michael would give cash in hand to the soldiers in exchange for their passes covering the days he knew he could get away.

CHAPTER 22
TESTING THE PLAN

As Michael prepared to test his plan, he became more anxious. He wondered how long it would take before the officers issuing passes would discover the soldier to whom the pass was issued was still in the barracks and not out on the pass. He had further concerns whether the guards at the gates would recognize the passes that contained names other than his own.

These concerns were somewhat alleviated when one of the officers of his adopted regiment learned the full story and plight of this "invisible soldier." The officer marveled at his ingenuity and volunteered to help him in any way he could. To Michael this officer's voice was like a warm embrace in the chilly air.

Michael was now ready to put his plan to its initial test. His work at the stables and grooming the horses would free him for 2 days hence. He contacted one of the soldiers and suggested that he obtain a 1-day pass covering the day that he knew he would be free. The deal was made. When Michael received the pass, the soldier would receive his $.75.

Michael spent the next day in a state of controlled excitement. Though his plan hinted of danger, it had exciting implications.

The pass was obtained by the soldier and turned over to Michael for the $.75 that had been promised. The next morning a strange, cold excitement filled his whole being as he shaved and dressed himself for the adventure of the day.

Michael waited patiently for a group of five or six soldiers with day passes to approach the guard's gate at the entrance to the camp. He was surprised and somewhat thrilled by his own behavior as he held up his pass for the guards to see and then proceeded through the open gate. He realized, with numb astonishment, that the guards at the gate did not check individual passes, and he hoped this would be the same procedure on his return.

As he walked down the country road toward the city of

Carlisle, he saw a train chuffing out its cloud of smoke and steam. It was then that he recalled Carlisle was about halfway between Philadelphia and Pittsburg and that he had ridden the train, many times before his enlistment, to visit friends in Pittsburg.

As he smelled the fresh country morning air, his mind drifted back to the raw smell of the good earth of his home in Germany. Memories opened before him as if a curtain had been ripped aside, but now he was free to think and do as he pleased. It was freedom, pure and simple.

With these thoughts, he smiled as he realized that this was truly the first freedom he had had since originally joining the army. He intended to make the most of it.

He thought first he would locate the train station to check on the schedule to and from Pittsburg. Unfortunately, there was no train station. He was disappointed to discover that although there was a train track between Carlisle and Harrisburg, it was only a spur and primarily used by the army as needs arose.

Michael also learned that Harrisburg was the capital of Pennsylvania and had been so since 1812. Harrisburg was on the rail line between Philadelphia and Pittsburg. It was slightly less than 100 miles to Philadelphia and it was 205 miles to Pittsburg. Michael welcomed this information for future use, as he began figuring the time it would take to make the trip from Carlisle to Pittsburg or Philadelphia. He already knew the trains traveled at approximately 15 to 20 miles an hour depending on the incline of the track.

But for now, how to get the 20 miles or more to Harrisburg became his latest problem. He could walk but that would take at least 7 hours and more than his day pass would permit. While wandering in town, he encountered a coach service that made daily round trips to Harrisburg. The schedule showed the coach left at 8 a.m. and arrived in Harrisburg shortly after 10 a.m. The return from Harrisburg left at 3 p.m. and arrived in Carlisle shortly after 5 p.m., in time for dinner, or in Michael's case, in time to get back to camp on a day pass.

Michael had already missed the 8 a.m. departure to Harrisburg but learned that most of the time there were seats available on the coach and that reservations were really only needed on weekends, that is, Friday through Sunday night returns.

Michael returned to camp much the same way he had left, among a group of four or five other soldiers who merely held up their passes as they proceeded through the guard gate. They returned in time for mess call.

As Michael lay awake on his bed that night, he mulled over the day's activities. This was a most restless night as his mind was tormented by the question: "Will I be caught in the web of my own weavings?"

CHAPTER 23

THE ADJUTANT GENERAL CALLING

In a partial dream state Michael was nudged fully awake by the company sergeant telling him the adjutant general wished to see him after mess call.

As he buttoned his flannel shirt, Michael had a short burst of disconnected thoughts. The reason the adjutant general wished to see him stood in front of the morning, killing all joy. He did not appear to be quite the "invisible soldier" that he had thought.

After eating, Michael proceeded as ordered. As usual, the adjutant general was very busy and Michael had to wait until he was called. Waiting didn't help Michael's mental anguish because of what he anticipated he might be told.

Finally he was called into the adjutant's office. As the general picked up the file on Michael and began reading it, Michael swallowed hard. He felt relieved when the general offered a small smile in Michael's direction. While the report was not complete, it was now obvious to the general that mistakes had been made by army personnel on his enlistment. He had been incorrectly assigned to the volunteer regiments rather than the regular army. The paperwork showed that he had enlisted for a full 5 years and only 3 of those 5 years had been served.

The general spoke in apologetic tones as he informed Michael that such mistakes were not uncommon because of the large number of volunteers that had stepped forward at the start of the Mexican-American War. He added that further investigation was necessary concerning the amount of money the U.S. Army owed him for his time in service.

This had to be checked out thoroughly with the volunteer regiment's commanders to determine if any monies had been advanced to him. The general was sorry that it would take a while longer for this investigation but suggested Michael continue handling this time in a manner in which the U.S. Army would be made proud and asked that he be patient just a little while longer.

Not enjoying his earlier thoughts and feelings of danger, Michael now let out a quiet exhale of relief. He was happy that some things had been worked out but was not completely happy with the 2 years he had left to serve in the army.

When the general asked him how he had been surviving army life at the Carlisle barracks, Michael explained that he had been moving from returning regiment to returning regiment for his billeting and mess requirements and had found activities to keep himself occupied. Michael confided nothing further to the general. The general seem satisfied and told Michael he would be back in touch with him when the payee requirements had been authenticated. With a salute and a thank-you, Michael returned to his morning duties.

For the next few days Michael continued cleaning stalls and grooming horses. That volunteer cavalry unit was to be mustered out by the end of the week, and a new unit being returned for processing would be arriving early the next week. Michael felt that his luck had been made in heaven. He could get a pass for 3 days for this weekend and return just in time to report to the new unit.

He pulled out all stops to get his 3-day pass. He wondered if the unit might be mustered out before the effective date of the pass and if that would be noticed by anyone or cause any concern. From his past experience he felt that it was not a major concern since passes were being given so freely.

Michael made his deal for the 3-day pass and now had the pass in hand. His attention turned to scheduling his transportation. This was to be the longest that he had been away from the army since joining, and he had high hopes that everything would work out as planned.

CHAPTER 24
OFF TO PITTSBURG

Michael was up early Friday morning and on his way to Carlisle before the crack of dawn. He realized this was a rather foolhardy venture since he would only have a short period of time in Pittsburg. This was due to the time it would takc to get there and get back before his pass expired. Nonetheless he had dreamed of this visit since meeting that special damsel on his previous journeys to Pittsburg before his army service.

He arrived in Carlisle to catch the 8 a.m. coach to Harrisburg. As planned, he purchased his ticket to Pittsburg on the 1 p.m. train, which would take about 18 hours of travel time and arrive at its destination at 7 a.m. the following morning.

As was customary, he purchased a number of food items to sustain himself during this long trip. After adhering to the early reveille calls and the long days of army life, he welcomed the extra hours of sleep and the interesting dreams that sleep always seemed to bring.

Michael felt refreshed and alive as he stepped off the train, in a state of controlled excitement. He hurried to the marketplace in time to help some of the vendors set up. He had just finished with one and was starting with another what he looked up and took a quick breath of utter astonishment. Walking toward him was the one he had come to see: the girl of his dreams. Her stride carried its own excitement. As she drew closer, she blinked in astonished silence. The way she looked almost made Michael's breath leave his body.

She opened her arms and he fell into them. They looked at one another with disbelief and enchantment. The memory of their time together years earlier ruffled through her mind like wind on water, and the floodgates of the past opened as they picked up the string of time.

They sat on a grassy area in the shade of the tree on the outskirts of the market as Michael explained his uniform and his time in the service. As they continued to talk, Michael realized that he knew little about his dream girl other than that her name was Philomene and she was a servant to one of the local families.

She started to tell Michael her story but then told him it would have to wait since time was short and she must get back to her owners' home soon with the market goods she had been ordered to obtain or she would be punished.

Michael was disturbed by her statement and knew it would take more time than they had now for him to discover exactly what it truly meant.

Picking up the necessary items from the market, they hurried back toward her place of employment. Michael was enjoying the walk down the narrow lane when he observed through the sunny arch in the trees a large French-style farmhouse. Philomene quickly explained that was where she lived and worked. Michael gave a short whistle of surprise as he gazed on its elegance.

Philomene told Michael that she had some chores to do but would meet him as soon as she could get away, in an hour or so. She asked him to wait for her under the big oak tree at the top of the hill behind the house. With that she grasped the basket of fruit and vegetables Michael had been carrying and ran toward the villa, her skirt flying in the breeze.

It was almost noon before Philomene could join Michael. She brought with her some refreshing lemonade and a simple lunch to share.

Michael pressed her to explain her earlier statements about her owners' home and possible punishment for being late.

Philomene was reluctant to recount her story for fear of losing Michael's attention. Sensing this, Michael briefly told her of his dreams and the adventures that had brought him to the United States. Feeling more comfortable, Philomene confided in Michael that she was an indentured servant to the family living in the French villa below the hill they sat on.

The term "indentured servant" was new to Michael, and he asked her for further details. With a heavy sigh and tears swelling in her eyes, she agreed to tell him her full life story.

CHAPTER 25
PHILOMENE'S STORY

Philomene's story unfolded as follows:

I was born in 1827. The exact date, I do not know. My full name is Margaret Philomene Gardner. Margaret is what my current family calls me, but Philomene was what my mother called me. Both my mother and father were English and arrived in New Orleans a number of years before my birth. I'm not sure what my father's occupation was, but I do know that he worked hard. I remember him coming home at night very tired and with his hands, face, and clothing dirty from grime and sweat.

We lived on a narrow street that was often covered with the leavings of horses and water that was thrown out into the street from the individual homes.

My mother would not permit me to wander the streets of New Orleans. She felt it totally unsafe for a young girl to do so alone. I really don't remember much about my days growing up on the back streets of New Orleans. But I do recall we lived among other poor families such as ourselves.

I have not had any formal schooling and cannot read or write. What little I know I have learned in my present home.

When I was 13 years old, a cholera epidemic hit New Orleans and many people died, including my parents. Memories of the days leading up to their death still haunt me as well as the marks put on the front door of our home alerting the officials of death in the home.

I was devastated when my parents' bodies were removed from the house and tossed on a wagon headed for burial, and our blankets and clothing were taken to be burned. I remember my younger brother, with tears streaming down his face, as the wagon rounded the corner at the end of the street.

We were alone in the house for the next several days eating what food we could beg from our poor neighbors. Some officials came and took us both away to another house in the better part of New Orleans where there were many other children. This was a frightening period for both my brother and me. We wondered what was to become of us.

We did not have long to wait. My brother and I were separated. He went with a family to live in California, I believe, and I was to go to a family living in Pittsburg, Pennsylvania. I had no idea where Pittsburg, Pennsylvania was but quickly learned that I would be put on a ship in New Orleans that would take me to Philadelphia, where someone would meet me and take me inland to Pittsburg.

That was a dreadful trip and I was sick most of the way. It was on that trip that I learned I was to become an indentured servant to a wealthy family in Pittsburg. I learned, also, what the term "indentured servant" actually meant. I was to work for them as they requested until the expenses for my ship travel and land travel to Pittsburg were reimbursed by my work. Additional expenses would be added for clothing as well as other necessary items. In considering this, I had no idea how long I would be working for this family. As you can see, I have now been here for about 8 years with no end in sight. I long to leave and make a life for myself, but my debt seems to be ever increasing.

As Philomene related this story, Michael could not help but think how their lives had experienced similar trials and tribulations in dreams of freedom of thought and action. Michael could not hide his tears as he visualized the situation Philomene had experienced.

Michael and Philomene sat motionless with their eyes on the ground as the story just related took its full effect. Philomene wondered if this story would change Michael's feelings toward her. Michael wondered if he had ever met a stronger woman.

CHAPTER 26
PONDERING PHILOMENE'S STORY

Time was drawing near for Michael's return to catch the 6 p.m. train back to Harrisburg, but he did not want to leave Philomene. She has been an indentured servant for this family for 8 years. Certainly that was long enough to have paid off the original bond, Michael thought. He also wondered what the original court-ordered bond contained.

He asked Philomene if she had ever seen any documents related to her enslavement. She told him she had not, and further emphasized she had never learned to read. This comment came as a shock to Michael, but as he thought about her situation, he began to understand.

Some way they must further investigate the whole matter. They decided that Philomene would seek information from those whom she trusted in the household while Michael would seek further understanding of the entire nature of the term "indentured servant."

Michael coached her to find out the original cost of bringing her to Pittsburg from New Orleans and how many work hours per diem would be applied against that charge. Also, what other charges might have been placed on her indebtedness over these past 8 years. They both felt this information would be difficult to obtain but that it was imperative in determining their next move.

With that final thought, Michael kissed Philomene good-bye and told her he would be back in a week or two, depending on his army duties. "Whatever the case, or delay, do not lose heart. I *will* return," Michael told her as he turned to hurry to the train station.

Michael arrived, breathless and without a minute to spare, as the train was loading and about to depart. He took a seat as far as possible from the other passengers. He needed time to collect himself and his thoughts. So much had happened within the past few hours that his mind was a whirl.

What exactly is an "indentured servant," and what are the laws governing the pay, the control, and the individual's rights and the length of service? He had so many questions and so few answers.

After he ate the meal Philomene had prepared for his long journey back to camp, he curled up in his seat and closed his eyes. His many thoughts wrecked his sleep and brought terror to his dreams. Finally sleep pushed away these teasing problems and he slid into a thin sleep.

He awoke suddenly to a carelessly drunken reply apparently being given to the train conductor who was directing an individual to sit down and be quiet. Michael quickly had to withdraw his feet from the seat to make room for this rather large unruly man. The smell of alcohol exploded from his mouth with every word he spoke. He had just boarded the train at the last station and would now be Michael's companion for the rest of the trip to Harrisburg.

Michael found it difficult to fall back to sleep, especially with the open-mouthed snoring and the odor of his new seat partner. Hours later, they were jerked fully awake by the jousting of the train through a rocky gorge on uneven tracks. As the conductor passed by, Michael inquired as to how much longer to Harrisburg. He was told about 2 hours.

It wasn't long before both men were fully awake and began to discuss the rough train ride. Shortly, Michael and his seat partner were sharing the leftovers of the meal Philomene had prepared and found themselves in deep conversation on other subjects. Michael learned his seat partner was a traveling man representing a large mercantile and furniture supplier based in Harrisburg and was now returning home. He further learned some of his contacts were with the larger plantations and mansions. Michael saw his opportunity and quickly directed the conversation to indentured servants.

His seat partner was well acquainted with indentured servants, one or two young women in particular, he told Michael with a devilish grin.

"By law," the seat partner told Michael, "unless otherwise stated in the original bonding of the individual, women must be released at age 18 and men at age 21."

Additionally, he told Michael, there was an established limit for adding costs for clothing, medical care, and other incidentals to the original bonding amount that the indentured servant may need from time to time. That limit varied somewhat by practice, area, and jurisdiction. He further mentioned that some unscrupulous holders of the bond add these costs in extreme amounts in order to extend the length of service necessary to pay off the bond amount. In his travels he had run into indentured servants who, he thought, would never earn their way out of their bondage because of this practice.

Michael fell silent while he considered these latest comments and how they might concern Philomene. As the train pulled into Harrisburg, Michael was more determined than ever to rescue Philomene from the captivity and servitude of her bondage.

CHAPTER 27

DREAMS OF LIFE WITH PHILOMENE

On his return to camp, Michael found nothing had changed and he had not been missed. He quickly discovered that there was no news from the adjutant general concerning either his future or his pay for past service.

During the day, he went about the normal routine he had established to earn money. The monotonous days passed slowly. His mind often drifted into a fuzzy haze. Nights were filled with loneliness and every nerve leaped and shattered as he thought about Philomene's predicament. Sleep and dreams came slowly as he thought about a future life with Philomene. Again and again, he relived their time together under the big oak tree and he clearly pictured her lovely, wide, warm smile and her passionate kiss good-bye.

Sleep came slowly each night, allowing his subconscious to surface and take command of his dreams. His mind continually tumbled through the details of Philomene's story and various ways he could help deliver her from her dilemma.

Each day he awoke with a confusing rush of anticipation but found only that the waves of grayness had not left him. He found little relief in cleaning stalls and grooming the horses. Throughout the day his jaw became firmer, his muscles tightened, and his heart grew more eager to find a solution. His work ethic began to suffer and did not go unobserved by his fellow soldiers. They reminded him that one must be fully alert and cautious while working around horses and mules.

But the warning came too late.

As Michael entered the stall of one of the pack mules, he pushed the mule to the side of the stall. The pack mule reacted to the push with a kick of his hind legs that struck Michael in the left arm and upper left chest. Two other soldiers working in nearby stalls observed this and ran to help Michael as he lay on the ground not fully aware of what had happened.

It was determined that Michael's injury could not be taken lightly, and the two soldiers proceeded to help Michael to the infirmary.

Michael's pride was hurt far worse than his physical body, although the doctor suspected a cracked rib. Michael took the doctor's advice and moved very little for the next few days while he convalesced. He found the nursing staff to be very attentive, warm, and helpful. He became aware of how conscientious the nurses were with their patients and recognized the glimmer of a relationship that he had felt with Philomene.

He tried to discipline his voice to maintain complete control, as he asked one of the nurses to share her story with him. She sat down next to his bed, took a deep breath, and plunged into the story of her life as a nurse. Over the next few days, the nurse came back to his bedside for further conversation and clarification of her job. During one of these conversations, Michael described Philomene to the nurse and asked if she thought, at least from his description of her, if Philomene might fulfill the requirements of a nurse or at least a nurse's assistant. The nurse told him that, judging from his description, Philomene would definitely be a good candidate.

Michael then questioned her about the possibilities of Philomene receiving nurses training at this infirmary or another that was located nearby. The nurse told him that it was possible but that they must meet her in person to determine her potential.

Michael felt as if a weight had been lifted off his back. Hopefully, this may develop into the solution to Philomene's dilemma. Only time would tell.

CHAPTER 28
BACK TO PITTSBURG

Michael's injuries from the mule kick and his stay in the infirmary were a thing of the past. He could now look to the future.

He engaged in his work with new vigor and enthusiasm. The money he earned cleaning stalls and grooming horses would serve him well for an early trip to Pittsburg and into the arms of Philomene. It was not difficult for him to wrangle another extended pass that would permit him to do just that.

Michael felt more comfortable on this trip than he had previously, and he was determined to spend his time wisely on the dismal long trip to Pittsburg. As he boarded the train in Harrisburg, he quickly searched for what he thought would be an appropriate seat partner. He wanted all additional information that he could get about indentured servants. The first seat partner that he selected either was not well informed or did not care to discuss the matter. At the next stop, Michael selected another candidate for information and was not disappointed. During their long discussions he learned some new facts that he believed would serve him well later.

He learned that when one had served his or her term of bondage, he or she would be entitled to a new suit of clothes at the parting. In addition, if it had been so stipulated, a man would get an additional horse, a woman, and a cow.

He further learned that in 1850 the U.S. Congress had passed the Fugitive Slave Act, which his seat partner thought also included indentured servants. Under this Act, slave hunters were allowed to capture an escapee, either slave or indentured servant, and confirm only orally before a state or federal judge that the person was a runaway. A hefty penalty of $1,000 was brought on anyone refusing to return the runaway. In addition, the runaway could be fined $1,000, which would be added to their bondage. Neither the indentured servant nor slave could ask for a jury trial or testify on his or her behalf. Any person aiding a runaway by providing shelter, food, or other assistance was liable to 6 months' imprisonment and a $500 fine. It was thought that the Fugitive Slave Act would diminish the incentive for slaves or indentured servants to escape. Even if they managed to escape, they could still be caught and returned by any citizen in the United States.

Michael's head was filled with weary thoughts as he finally closed his eyes and tried to sleep. This new information altered somewhat his plan for Philomene and prompted him to begin devising a new plan that might circumvent the penalties that had been described.

New thoughts continued to rack his sleep and terrorize his dreams. It was finally morning and just a few hours before reaching Pittsburg, he finally slid into a light sleep. Shortly thereafter, he awoke with sudden anxiety and the impatience of a challenger. He dismissed his nightmares of the previous evening and rose with conviction for what he now knew he must do.

CHAPTER 29
PURSUING THE PLAN

As before, Michael hurried to let Philomene know of his arrival. He found her doing her daily shopping in the market and asked her to meet him at the top of the hill as soon as she could. He would be waiting.

He did not have long to wait. Philomene arrived within the hour with a smile on her face and a basket of fresh fruit and some chunks of cheese. This was most welcomed by Michael since he had not had breakfast.

Michael asked her what she had learned of her bondage since their last meeting and she related not a great deal. She had learned that the amount owed was approximately $80 but did not know on what basis this amount had been determined.

This amount took Michael by surprise. Philomene had become an indentured servant at age 13 and was now 21. These 8 years at 6 cents a day would amount to well over the current debt. This meant her transportation from New Orleans to Pittsburg should be covered by her past labor. He then told Philomene that he had learned that an indentured child was to be released at age 18 by most laws that had been established and asked if she'd heard anything about this from her investigation. She replied she had not. It became apparent that the 3 years of servitude after age 18 at a minimum 6 cents per day would be close to fulfilling the $80 now required.

They continued to discuss the other points Michael had discovered and began to wonder if it was even wise to attempt discussing the matter further with the man she referred to as "Master." Over the years he had treated her rather kindly but never as part of the family. The rudimentary service and cleaning functions of the manor house had mostly been performed by Philomene. She felt somewhat indebted to him and the family for taking her in after both of her parents had died. While she did not believe that he would cause a problem with her now leaving her bondage, she was not completely sure because he was considered by many in the community as a miser.

Over the next hour or so, they considered what to do next.

Master had drive, a temper, and shrewd intuitions. In addition, he insisted on ruling with a firm hand over all his lower socially positioned servants. He was a man who did not like to be outmaneuvered, and Philomene had seen him, at times, as uncompromising and totally unbearable.

They both agreed that the Master was someone they did not wish to anger in any way. Additionally Michael felt he would not be able to hold his own in any discussion or debate with him concerning Philomene's welfare. This reality led them to only one conclusion: Philomene must run away with Michael at the earliest possibility and with little fear of what might happen if she were to be classified as a true runaway, captured, and forced to return to the manor house. With such a realization they both swallowed hard and looked longingly in each other's eyes. Philomene recognized Michael's face betrayed a certain tension, a secret passion held rigidly under control. Michael was thinking of the four freedoms that caused him to leave home years before – the freedoms of expression and belief and the freedoms from want and from fear – and how they applied again now.

Philomene was to return to her normal duties for the rest of the morning but find time to put aside a few of her personal items to be gathered up in a bundle later in the afternoon. It sounded simple: Michael would meet her outside the Manor House in late afternoon, after her chores were done for the day, and the two of them would proceed to the train station to connect with the 6 p.m. train to Harrisburg.

CHAPTER 30
COMPLETING THE ESCAPE

Philomene felt numb as she placed a bundle of her clothes near the spot where she was to meet Michael. She had only sensed love at a far distance, never daring to approach it. The feelings she had now were beyond anything that she had ever encountered. She felt aggressive and alive yet in a state of controlled excitement as she prepared to leave one lifc for an exciting new one.

Dusk covered the hills with a purple mist as Michael and Philomene walked alert, cautiously and silently in the half light of the night as it began swooping over the village. Michael went to the ticket window alone to purchase the needed extra ticket for the return trip to Harrisburg. He related the need to the fact he had lost his return ticket and scolded himself for being so careless. He then returned to Philomene, who was hiding in the shadows and rushed into the waiting car just as the train started to leave. They sat in the back corner of the coach with the shade half pulled in hopes that no one acquainted with Philomene would observe her.

As the train gathered speed and left the city behind, they looked warily at one another as if they were condemned criminals. Their wariness turned to smiles that grew broader until they both let out a little chuckle. The floodgate had opened and the torment of the past few hours had found its way out.

The trip back to Harrisburg was uneventful while Michael and Philomene both drifted into deep, satisfying sleep. They awoke as the train slowed for the stop in Harrisburg.

Stepping off the train, Michael searched the platform for any indication that Philomene's escape may have been forwarded for the station master to be on the lookout. Seeing nothing out of the ordinary, they moved quickly for their connection to Carlisle and Michael's return to camp before his pass expired. He realized he was cutting his return close to being late. Everything must happen as planned, and there must be no unanticipated problems or delays.

CHAPTER 31

THE OUTSIDE HELP

As Michael and Philomene approached the entry gate to the camp, Michael observed the shadowy figure he was hoping to see standing just outside the gate. As promised, the nurse who had previously cared for him was waiting.

After a brief introduction, she took Philomene by the hand and walked through the gate observed but unchallenged. Michael joined a group of returning soldiers and together they passed through the gate holding up their passes as they went by the guards.

So far his plan had worked perfectly. The nurse took Philomene to the nurse's residence near the infirmary and would seek immediate approval for Philomene's acceptance into nurses training. Michael returned to his normal routine at the camp with the hope that his situation would not change before Philomene completed her training.

Philomene and Michael saw each other frequently during the next few weeks. Philomene's training was moving forward quickly, and she found it not only fascinating but enjoyable. She told Michael that the training nurse was impressed with her work and recognized that she took to it like a duck to water. Michael received this information with a sigh of relief since he had been somewhat concerned with the plan.

Michael was becoming impatient with the delay from the adjutant general's office, which continued to affect any future planning for his and Philomene's life together. He decided to check with the office in the next day or so. Their investigation had been going on for months. Even his army buddies were beginning to refer to him as the "invisible" or "forgotten" soldier.

His visit proved fruitful, at least, to some degree. He was told that the investigation had been completed and that the only thing remaining was the amount he was to be paid and whether he owed any time to the length of service for which he had originally enlisted. Both of these facts should be determined within the next few weeks and that they would send a "runner" for him at that time.

CHAPTER 32
THE DAY OF JUDGMENT

Michael did not have long to wait. A runner came to get him for a consultation with the adjutant general. His whole body tightened when he heard this request, and he took a short uneasy breath and followed the runner back to headquarters.

The room where he was to meet the adjutant general was filled with at least five officers. After a slight hesitation, he entered the room. The officers looked warily from one to the other and exchanged quick glances at Michael as he reported as ordered. The adjutant general seemed somewhat different than he had observed on previous visits. Michael looked at him straight on, hoping for some soothing words.

Every nerve in Michael's body tensed as he waited for the adjutant general to speak. The subject of Michael's desertion was still on the table. Punishment for desertion was a year in prison, loss of pay, reduction in rank, dishonorable discharge.

The general spoke softly as he reiterated what they discovered concerning Michael's service in the Mexican-American War. The general continued at some length, often referring to various documents that he had been provided by the officers under which Michael had served. All had given Michael glowing reports as to his bravery, his commitment, and his involvement in various battles, especially noting San Juan Hill and the capture of the Mexican general, Santa Anna. Hearing this, the other officers in the room began to smile and issue congratulatory words to this "veteran."

The adjutant general announced that Michael had not been a deserter but rather a hero who had inadvertently served with the Pennsylvania Volunteer Regiment rather than the U.S. Army in which he had officially enlisted. He further recognized that Michael had not been paid for his 2 years, 11 months in service. Therefore, Michael was to receive payment for these 35 months at the going rate of $8 per month, thus making a total of $280 being owed to Michael as of this day. This amount would be made available to Michael on his visit to the quartermaster payroll officer.

The next announcement made by the adjutant general was not quite as Michael had hoped. Because Michael had originally signed his name on enrollment documents for the U.S. Army for a period of 5 years, he must now serve an additional 2 years and 1 month in keeping with this original commitment. He was to stay with the cavalry infantry unit with whom he had been serving for these past
few months.

Michael's patience, though difficult to maintain, had been rewarded. Finally his future was clearer and his understanding of the freedom, the truthfulness, honesty, and fairness of the United States was confirmed, once again. He hurried to tell Philomene.

CHAPTER 33
THE EXCITEMENT BUILDS

Michael had a difficult time finding Philomene in any of her usual places. He finally found her at the hospital with a female patient. As she turned to meet Michael, he noted her face was flushed and damp with perspiration. Philomene brushed her hair from her eyes and faced Michael to give him her latest news. Michael, however, was first and loudest with the news of his new freedom. Philomene listened but did not hear him. She was going over and over her own news for him.

Then the drug of calm took over and they looked at each other and smiled. They walked out of the hospital toward Philomene's home in silent contemplation. Finally Michael took a deep breath and broke into an easy laugh. Michael recognized she had something important to share with him.

She did indeed! The woman Michael had seen her with in the hospital had just given birth and Philomene was the birthing midwife. This was the first time she had performed the service unaided and unsupervised. She was advancing in her medical education much faster than either she or the training nurses had ever anticipated. Michael congratulated her for this achievement, and Philomene beamed with pride.

Michael reiterated his news more fully. These announcements to each other were astonishing and filled them with thoughts and expectations for their near future.

A few days later, Michael received official orders that he was to join his current unit, just as he had been previously told by the adjutant general. Additionally, he was to prepare to leave with them for deployment on the Minnesota Territory frontier.

He had a couple of weeks to prepare for this new assignment. First in Michael's mind was to collect the $280 owed him for past service. He hurried to the paymaster before the commitments by the adjutant general would be forgotten.

Payment was made accordingly, and Michael held in his

hand more money than he had ever anticipated. When he showed this new wealth to Philomene, she gasped. “Now we can get married,” Michael blurted out, then blinked in astonishment at his audacity. He looked inquiringly at Philomene. His comment made Philomene’s breath leave her body but was quickly followed by a curious tingling feeling as she replied, “Yes, oh yes!”

CHAPTER 34
THE ARMY TO THE RESCUE

Michael learned quickly that a great deal of preparation was necessary for his outfit to leave for the Minnesota frontier. The preparation must include his proposal and Philomene's response. Time was fleeting!

Preparation from the army's standpoint moved quickly and efficiently while Michael agonized over his own personal preparation. However, when Michael discovered that his outfit would be moving through Pittsburg, his plan began to take form.

He hurried to the hospital to visit with the nurse who had been so helpful with Philomene's training. He explained his predicament in detail and received a smile of understanding and a solution far greater than he had anticipated.

Michael felt a bursting of magic bubbles in his head as the nurse proposed that she would recommend Philomene to accompany the outfit as part of the medical unit. Philomene was ready for new responsibilities, the training nurse told Michael, and she felt sure her proposal would be received readily and without reservation. She told Michael not to worry and instead to focus on the fact that Philomene had agreed to marry him.

The next time Michael and Philomene were together, she told him that she had been assigned to the medical unit of Michael's outfit, just as the nurse had proposed. When Michael related that the unit would be going through Pittsburg with a stay of perhaps a couple of days, Philomene was delighted. Although she had run away from her indentured servitude without so much as a good-bye or thank-you, she suggested they marry in Pittsburg, among her friends and acquaintances.

New problems quickly entered Michael's mind. How could this be arranged? How would the Master react to Philomene's return, and how would he exercise any rights he might have under the law?

Michael sought help from his commanding officer the very next day. On hearing this whole story and Michael's desire to get married in Pittsburg, the captain suggested they obtain legal advice from the adjutant general.

The adjutant general remembered the "invisible soldier" immediately and listened intently as Michael again related this story. After asking a few questions, the adjutant general sat in deep thought with a finger on his cheek and his thumb holding up his chin. Finally, he turned to Michael and the captain with his conclusions:

Number 1: By law, Philomene's indentured servitude should have ended when she reached age 18. She was held illegally for an additional 3 years.

Number 2: Philomene is now a U.S. Army nurse and is beyond civilian legal jurisdiction.

Number 3: Michael Myers, Philomene's supposed abductor, is a U.S. Army soldier and likewise is beyond civilian legal jurisdiction.

Number 4: On receipt of the name and address of her previous debt holder, I personally will write and relate these conclusions and further request the two of you meet to resolve any remaining details as your army unit passes through Pittsburg in a week or two. This letter will be sent by U.S. Army dispatch to ensure early arrival.

Michael promised delivery of the name and address before sunset. One concern remained in Michael's mind. Would the Pittsburg layover provide enough time for Philomene and Michael to be married as she had wished? Only time would tell!

CHAPTER 35
THE APPREHENSIVE RETURN

Empty boxcars were waiting in Carlisle as wagons from the camp began to arrive. Wagons, horses, and other equipment were loaded into designated empty boxcars. As the unmarried soldiers arrived, they were assigned to specific coach cars. Married soldiers and their wives and any family members were assigned to one of the remaining coach cars near the end of all the other cars. The final car was reserved for officers and their wives. Michael was in the coach with the unmarried soldiers, and Philomene was in the coach with the married soldiers and their wives.

The commanding officer made a last-minute check to ensure everything had been loaded properly and signaled the train engineer to hook up the engine and proceed on the trip to Harrisburg. The train arrived in Harrisburg and was switched and immediately picked up by another engine for their trip to Pittsburg.

During this rather long trip, both Michael and Philomene

talked to those around them about their hopes of getting married during the short stopover in Pittsburg. The women received Philomene's news with excitement. The soldiers took Michael's announcement with a blink of astonished silence, a smile of amusement, and a whistle or two of surprise.

The logistics of how this wedding was to actually happen weighed heavily on Michael's mind. After mulling this over, hour after hour as the train's clickety click on the railroad tracks drew them closer and closer to Pittsburg, Michael concluded that only fate would solve all related problems.

A short time after their early-morning arrival in Pittsburg, the captain, with a smile on his face, informed Michael that they would have approximately a 3-day layover as additional wagons and other equipment were obtained and loaded. He gave Michael a 3-day pass. Michael thanked the captain, and after saluting, he hurried off to find Philomene.

As they went through the market on the way to the Manor house to meet with the Master, Philomene spotted one of the indentured servants that she had worked beside for many years. Their excited chatter was hard for Michael to follow, but he concluded that the adjutant general's letter had been received and the Master was expecting Philomene's reappearance. Neither Michael nor Philomene was sure what that actually meant for their future together. The rush of anticipation and dread whirled inside Philomene, and Michael's body tensed. With every step toward the Manor house, Michael's jaw clenched, his muscles tightened, and his heart grew more eager to get this meeting over with.

Approaching the front door of the Manor house, Philomene paused. No indentured servant was ever permitted to enter through the front door. Awaiting Michael's knock on the door to announce their arrival, Philomene stood there as though fastened to the wall with her adrenaline level rising even higher. Michael took her hand in a firm grip as they waited for someone to answer the door. Surprise showed on the face of the servant girl as she opened the door and then, with a smile of recognition, she escorted them into the parlor. She then hurried to inform the Master of their arrival.

CHAPTER 36
THE ARBITRATION

As Philomene looked around the parlor, her whole body tightened and she took a deep breath. She moved closer to Michael and grabbed his arm tightly. She had never before been permitted to step foot in the parlor.

Shortly, the Master and his wife entered the room. Philomene's grip on Michael's arm tightened, and she moved slowly behind Michael's left shoulder for the protection she felt she needed. Her grip loosened as she observed the Master's smile and heard his words of welcome. He seemed pleased to see Philomene, and his greeting to Michael was cordial as he told Michael that he had looked forward to meeting him after receiving the adjutant general's recent letter.

Michael quickly observed the paper in the Master's hand and asked if that was an accounting of Philomene's servitude. The Master said it was and that he was now fully prepared to discuss it with Michael as the general had suggested.

It appeared that the daily maintenance costs of Philomene's living with the family far exceeded the legal payment required to be paid to indentured servants, leaving a balance owed of $60.

Michael immediately took exception to these charges stating Philomene had been a free woman at age 18 but was not notified of this freedom in order to make her own decision to stay or leave. While Michael expressed his thanks to the family for having provided Philomene with a home these approximately 3 years after the legal limit of her servitude, it was still unlawful and would not hold up in a court of law.

The Master's expression changed somewhat as he studied Michael's statement and his apparent determination. Admitting that he had been wrong not to inform Philomene that her servitude was concluded at age 18, he proposed a settlement of half the $60.

Again complimenting him for the family's care of

Philomene during those 3 years, Michael stated that half of the half would be more appropriate.

Recognizing the consequences of his not agreeing with Michael's conclusion and with a deep sigh, the Master agreed. Michael quickly produce the $15 and the two shook hands with smiles on their faces, happy to have concluded the discussion so amiably.

A letter of understanding was prepared and given to Michael to safeguard Philomene's freedom from any future ramifications.

The Master's wife proposed they all sit down and celebrate with tea and crumpets. At first Philomene felt uncomfortable in the sitting room, which previously she had not been allowed to enter. This feeling was quickly put aside as the discussion turned to what had been happening in Philomene's life since she left the mansion. Shortly, the discussion turned to Philomene and Michael's future.

There was no hesitation in Michael's reply when he told them that within a day or so they were to be married. Smiles around the room greeted this announcement.

Michael then felt it appropriate to ask if their wedding ceremony could be held under the big oak tree at the top of the hill behind the mansion. The Master's wife confirmed, with enthusiasm, that they could and asked when they wanted their wedding to take place. Philomene, recognizing their army unit would only be there for a few more days, proposed, "Today if possible."

All that remained was getting final permission from Michael's commanding officer and finding someone to perform the ceremony.

The Master offered his coach to take them back to where Michael's outfit was bivouacked, and his wife offered to handle the site of the ceremony. Both Philomene and Michael graciously accepted, recognizing this total change in the relationship.

CHAPTER 37
THE WEDDING

Michael had no problem receiving special permission from the commanding officer to proceed with the wedding and was further assured when his C.O. promised he would do whatever he could to make it a memorable occasion. Word quickly spread throughout the army unit that their wedding was to take place at 5 p.m. that very day.

Meanwhile, back at the mansion, the Master and his wife were busy with the necessary details of the marriage. The Master sent word to the parson of his church that his services were required. The kitchen of the mansion was bustling with excitement as the cooks prepared light sandwiches, liquid refreshment, and a small assortment of pastries for the wedding guests. The other indentured servants were in a dither of excitement.

Makeshift tables were erected at the top of the hill under the big oak tree and surrounded by fresh flowers from the mansion's garden.

When Michael and Philomene arrived, they were astonished at the romantic transformation of their favorite meeting spot.

As the appointed time for the ceremony, many of their friends from Philomene's medical attachment and from Michael's mounted infantry unit began to arrive. Michael had expected a few of his closest friends to be in attendance, but he was wholly taken back by the number of guests that appeared. Even his commanding officer was present. A lot of bustle and ballyhoo erupted among the gathering as a team of horses pulling a wagon stopped at the far side of the old oak tree.

Michael's wonderment quickly subsided when the commanding officer told him the wagon was his until tomorrow noon. Michael's eyes quickly raked Philomene with a fiercely possessive look and she, feeling the power of his gaze, smiled in return. Stunned by the intensity of their vibes, both bride and groom flushed, then quickly began greeting their wedding guests.

A few of Michael's closest friends dragged him toward the covered wagon for a closer inspection. The wagon was empty except for a mattress pad and bedding they had requisitioned especially for the occasion. The wagon itself was new, having been purchased earlier in the day by the army. Michael was informed that his unit would be leaving Pittsburg the next afternoon and that the horses would return by 11 a.m. to pull the wagon back to the bivouac area where he would rejoin his outfit.

The ceremony concluded just as dusk began filling the hills with a purple mist and fiddle music by one of Michael's army buddies paid tribute to the couple. May 15, 1850: The end of a perfect day, and the beginning of a new life, together, with Philomene.

CHAPTER 38

OFF ON A NEW ADVENTURE

Philomene and Michael awoke to the smell of coffee. The accompanying smell of frying bacon entered the wagon, encouraging them to quickly dress and join Michael's army buddies who had arrived early with the horses to pull the wagon back to the bivouacked area. Breakfast was more of a wedding morning afterthought but one that the new husband and wife welcomed.

By mid-morning the horses were harnessed to the wagon, and the couple began the trip down the hill back to reality. Three or four of the remaining indentured servants waved vigorously while the wagon moved from under the big oak tree and disappeared down the far side of the hill.

Arriving at the bivouac area, the newlyweds reluctantly returned to their respective duties, which now included helping prepare the outfit for the long journey ahead. Their "Honeymoon Wagon" was promptly loaded with various medical items and other supplies, making it difficult for them to recall their happy experiences of the previous night.

It wasn't long before they learned that their army unit had been assigned to a new fort, recently constructed on the frontier in Minnesota Territory. The trip was to be an arduous journey that would include travel by wagon train, or railroads where such service existed. There might also be travel by boat. Because rail service ended at Pittsburg, the first stretch would be by wagon train. This would take them the 185 miles from Pittsburg to Crestline, Ohio in hopes of connecting with a new rail line, which would then take them farther west.

Shortly after lunch, the wagon train began moving. The travel was slow, dusty, and hot, giving them all an idea of what to expect. Because of their late start and their inexperience as travelers, they covered only 5 miles before stopping to make camp and have dinner.

The bugler awakened the camp shortly after sunrise. Within half an hour after breakfast, they moved out on the second leg of their journey. This routine would follow them through each day until they reached their final destination.

The monotony of the journey was broken only as they passed through the small Ohio settlements of Beaver, Salem, Canton, Wooster, and Loudonville, along the way.

With stops for lunch and short stays in various settlements, this 185-mile stretch took them close to a month to complete. Traveling 10 miles a day was the goal. This slow speed proved to be beneficial in at least one instance.

The bumping and shaking of the wagons as they traveled along the crude roads was too much for one of the pregnant wives. She could not hold off until the wagon train reached the next settlement.

Philomene was selected as the midwife to deliver the baby. She and Michael, along with the pregnant woman and her husband, were left behind and told to catch up with the outfit after the baby was born. One older horse and a small buckboard were left with them along with a few days of provisions. This was the army's usual practice in addressing such situations.

The next morning, with Philomene's help, the baby was born with no complications. The following morning, the new mother and baby were made comfortable on the buckboard, and the small group proceeded to reattach itself to the army unit, which now was approximately 2 days ahead.

With a terrible suddenness, the old horse, untrained as a harness horse, stepped in a gopher hole and broke one of its rear legs. There was nothing else to do but put the horse out of its misery, abandon the buckboard, and proceed on foot. However, there was one major problem. The new mother's boots and most of her clothing had remained in one of the wagons which were now days ahead of them.

With blankets and other materials found on the buckboard, Michael crafted a workable pair of boots for the new mother. After a day or so of walking over rough ground, however, these boots provided little protection. Her feet were bloodied by sharp rocks and from various prickly weeds along the way. She could walk no farther!

A travois, of sorts, was made and Michael and the woman's husband took turns pulling it. This slowed their travel speed, but they continued walking until darkness overtook them. They rose the next morning at the crack of dawn, in hopes of rejoining the outfit before midday.

As they reached the crest of one of the higher hills, they shouted with joy. They spotted the main unit not more than a mile ahead of them. They hastened their pace to reach the unit, knowing that it would be stopping for their lunch break.

Hot, sweaty, and exhausted, they entered the new bivouac area to cheers and welcoming greetings from their comrades and their wives. However, two officers that approached them were not smiling. "Where is the buckboard and the horse?" they asked.

Michael explained what happened and pointed to the new mother's bloody feet in an attempt to gain some sympathy.

No sympathy was given. The loss of the old horse was of no major consequence, but the loss of the buckboard would require compensation from the father of the new baby since he was to blame for the small group being left behind. His pay would be docked each month until a $30 reimbursement had been made to the U.S. Army.

Such is army life, they were told. “What about a little empathy?” Michael thought, as he stumbled on something he did not quite understand.

CHAPTER 39
WESTWARD HO

By the time lunch was over, word had circulated around camp of the $30 reimbursement payment the officers were requiring of the new father. Before the dinner stop, a hat was passed from wagon to wagon and soldier to soldier. With 25 cents here, 50 cents there and an occasional dollar, the soldiers gathered more than the $30 required.

Just before the final bugle call of the day, $30 was presented to the red-faced officers and the remainder went to the new father along with a receipt from the embarrassed officers.

Early the next morning, the doctor was attending to the new mother, her feet, and the new baby. The doctor ordered that she ride in one of newer, gentler wagons where she was to remain until her feet had fully recovered. Perhaps the officers had learned something beyond what had been taught in military school.

The journey continued without further incident, and the outfit arrived in Crestline, the railroad junction of a number of newly established railroads. In the next few days the soldiers were to load their wagons and equipment onto the provided boxcars for the next portion of their trip to the frontier.

It was about 100 miles from Crestline to Fort Wayne, Indiana, where they were to transfer to the Ohio and Indiana railroad line, which had just completed a connection to Fort Wayne and on to Chicago, Illinois. While their ordinance would be in the boxcars, they would be traveling in the passenger cars. This gave Michael and Philomene time to visit and discuss their future.

They learned that the Minnesota Territory was in a pre-railroad, pre-telegraph era and had not yet acquired the implements of civilization that its eastern neighbors already possessed. The territory was increasing its population and developing its resources at such a rate that it would soon cease to be a frontier and would become an established commonwealth.

Rivers were the chief avenues of travel, along with an

occasional ox cart that creaked across the prairies. Indian depredations had not been banished and that was the primary reason for the new fort that had recently been established and was now their final destination.

Additional information was gained from a book purchased in Fort Wayne, which described Zebulon Pike's travels to the Mississippi River's headwaters in 1805. The book contained stories about the aboriginal water craft of Minnesota's tribal people and of the tribal people themselves. Reading and discussing these stories made the many hours of the boring train travel pass more quickly and more enjoyably.

On their arrival in Chicago, Michael and Philomene learned the first building in the area had been built in 1780 by a fur trader and that the city now had a population of approximately 19,000 people. Less than 20 years previously, the Indian tribes of Chippewa, Pottawatomi, and Ottawa had agreed to cede their rights and were forced to move farther west. This permitted current settlers to flock to the area, which was now safe.

For the next 5 days, the army unit bivouacked just outside

the city. The soldiers were permitted numerous passes into the city during this time. Michael and Philomene were among the few who welcomed the news that they would be leaving. Neither liked the hustle and bustle of the big city.

Early the next morning, the wagon train pulled out and headed the 100 or so miles west toward the cities of Moline and Rock Island. Michael and Philomene were excited to learn that Rock Island was on the Mississippi River, and they began wondering, with much anticipation, about the new adventures that awaited them.

CHAPTER 40
MICHAEL'S FLASHBACKS

The trip from Chicago was uneventful, but seeing the huge Mississippi River was breathtaking and immediately brought back Michael's memories of his earlier river adventures.

The outfit bivouacked along the riverbank while they waited for the boats that would take them upriver. Two rather large rear paddle wheel boats arrived from St. Louis inside of a week. Within a couple of days, the boats were loaded with the wagons, animals, and passengers. As the boats pulled out from Rock Island, the captain of each boat ordered five long blasts of the ships' horns to be sounded as a departing gesture. The locals remaining on the banks waved and shouted best wishes and good luck. The soldiers and their wives waved back their thanks.

Michael was intrigued with the rear paddle wheel since the boat that he had served on when he crossed the Atlantic had contact with several crew members who offered to give him a personal tour of the vessel after they had performed their duties.

Michael knew their duties would include stoking the fire while his would include cleaning the horse stalls. There was plenty of time between these duties for them to get together, since the trip upriver would take a couple of weeks, at best.

As the days passed, Michael learned much about Fort Snelling, their immediate destination, the river, and the land of Minnesota itself. The first stern-wheeler to reach Fort Snelling had arrived in 1823. The river was still thc chief avenue of travel and immigration, but ox carts still creaked across the prairies and fear of Indian depredations had not yet dissipated.

The earlier pioneers discussed the prospects for statehood. Town sites appeared overnight and land speculators were everywhere. Statehood would still be a distant event. It was fortunate that they would arrive before winter set in since upstream rivers necessary to their travel would be cut off by ice until spring.

As their stern-wheeler passed various settlements and Indian villages, they saw a variety of Indian bark canoes, skin boats, and simple rafts. Michael was intrigued by the river and was up early each morning to observe flatboats being dragged upstream by hand. He was brought up sharply as they passed a lumber camp and watched carefully as log rafts arrived there. He recalled his own adventures guiding similar log rafts down the Rhine River.

As the stern-wheeler proceeded upriver, Michael waved vigorously to each man guiding a log raft and enthusiastically shared with Philomene and others just how dangerous and deadly such an occupation can be.

Michael had further stories to share after his visit with the ship's crew members and his tour of the engine room. He learned it was no longer necessary for an individual to physically enter the boiler to effect its cleaning. Science had removed that necessity in the past few years. The boiler on this steamship was a great deal smaller than the one on the *Rotterdam Westphalia,* which he and Hans had to periodically clean on their trip to America.

While the trip upriver seemed almost like a vacation, of

sorts, everything came to an abrupt close on their arrival at Fort Snelling. The first individuals they met were rough boatmen, coarse and violent frontiersmen, and whiskey-drinking Indians. Adventuring alone outside the fort was ill advised.

CHAPTER 41
ADVENTURING INTO THE UNKNOWN

Michael was intrigued by what he saw and was eager to experience what he expected to be very different from his life in America so far.

After finishing his duties for the day, he was free to wander the old fort and visit with some of the ruffians he had observed on his outfit's arrival. He found them quite willing, even eager, to share their stories with him. He felt comfortable with them and they apparently with him. They talked well into the late afternoon, pausing only for an occasional sip of some God-forsaken rotgut whiskey. When Michael heard "mess call," he excused himself and promised to seek them out again soon. As he stood up, he nearly fell over. Gathering his hat and jacket, he staggered home to Philomene.

Philomene had never seen Michael in such condition. Nonetheless, she greeted him with a smile and a strong right arm to support him. After dinner, Michael explained to her what he had learned and his interest in learning even more.

Days turned into weeks as Michael sought out his new friends to hear more of their stories. He became convinced that the Indians were reacting no differently than he would in similar conditions or situations imposed on them. He was determined to seek out some Indians with whom to speak, to further his knowledge of their plight.

His opportunity came when his outfit, Company A, 6th U.S. Infantry, left the safety of Fort Snelling for their assignment at Fort Ripley in central Minnesota Territory. They became the post's first garrison when they arrived on April 13, 1849.

Michael sought out one of the Indian scouts that had been assigned to accompany their outfit to the new location. Through the scout he learned that Chief Little Crow had led an attack on white settlers at the Lower Sioux Agency and that the Indian trader Andrew Myrick had been one of the first white men killed. He had tried to escape through a second floor window. His body was found days later, with grass stuffed in his mouth. The provisions of the agency were taken, and several buildings at the site were torched. At least 44 deaths occurred that day; 24 soldiers were killed, 5 were wounded, and only 16 survived. Learning this, Michael was concerned about taking Philomene into such an environment.

As they traveled toward their new destination, Michael further learned that the Sioux were continuing their rampage, attacking white settlements throughout the area. Finally some good news was unearthed. Dakota warriors decided not to attack the heavily defended Fort Ridgely along the river, instead turning toward the town of New Ulm. Unknown to them, the residents had organized defenses in the town center and kept the Dakotas at bay.

Despite Indian problems throughout the area, settlements began to spring up all across the vast Minnesota Territory. Minnesota was not nearly as civilized as areas to the east, but its population was growing rapidly and soon it would no longer be part of the wild west but rather more of an established commonwealth.

Michael further learned of the broken promises, fraudulent dealings, and encroachment of the settlers on Indian lands in spite of the many treaties that had been signed by the government of the United States.

Michael's recall of his own plight in the loose confederacy of Germany in years gone by made him sympathetic to that of the Indians. He determined, then and there, to do what he could with all future contacts with Indians by taking an offensive stand with a total understanding of their feelings.

This new determination was to cause some major conflicts of duty for Michael. He was a cavalry infantry soldier, assigned there on the frontier, to protect white settlers against Indian attacks.

CHAPTER 42
THE CONFLICT

On finishing his daily chores, Michael sat quietly by himself, pondering these new feelings. He awoke in the morning with a troubled mind. How was he to handle these combined roles, the first of being an infantry soldier ordered to kill Indians who were merely fighting to protect their heritage; the other, the deep-seated thoughts he held close to his heart since youth and his activities with the Freedom Fighters? His mind whirled with a conglomerate of thoughts.

With the practiced eye of one who had lived many years in servitude, Philomene recognized Michael's plight. Michael was a deeply caring man who now found himself in the wrong job. He now had a vested interest in the chaos of the Indian wars.

Michael and his wife talked late into the night, straight talk with simple answers, as they formulated their strategy. The talk progressed from Michael's need to create trouble and pressure to the fundamental reality of the situation.

As they finally headed for bed, they thought he would be damned if he did and damned if he didn't. There was little way out without truly upsetting his duty and/or his and Philomene's life.

Morning provided some relief and some fresh new thoughts. He could go with his outfit to confront Indians and pretend to shoot to kill but use only blank cartridges. He would appear to be performing his duties as a soldier yet still preserve his conviction to do no harm. As he further mulled over his thoughts, he determined he would be living a lie and be unsupportive of the other soldiers as they performed their duties.

A new idea occurred to him. He could request a transfer from the infantry to a noncombatant function of his outfit. This might include duties in the mess hall or in the medical division. He quickly dismissed this idea since it indicated cowardice. Because they knew about his Mexican-American War record, his present commanding officers would see through this ruse.

For the next few days, the question remained answered. Michael's outfit had not been called to action against the Indians, but that was destined to change shortly.

CHAPTER 43
THE SOLUTION

Philomene heard the news first. Captain Valentine Trant McGillycuddy, the commanding officer of the hospital unit in which she served, had just been appointed the Indian agent for the area served by the fort. She obtained a copy of the orders and showed it to Michael. Michael read these orders with wonderment.

The average Indian agent's duties are as follows:

>Work toward preventing conflicts between settlers and Indians.

>Keep an eye out for violations of intercourse laws and report them to superintendents in Washington.

>Maintain flexible cooperation with U.S. Army military personnel.

>See to the proper distribution of amenities granted by the

state or federal government to various Indian tribes; this usually occurs through the transfer of money or goods from the Indian agent to the respective chief who then distributes them to the tribe.

>Oversee the successful removal of tribes from areas procured for white settlements and successful transfer of tribes to reservations.

Michael read and reread these duties, paying a special interest to the third one. Somewhere in these duties, Michael conjured up a solution to his quandary. After further discussion with Philomene, they decided a meeting with Captain McGillycuddy was in order. Philomene was to seek an appointment for Michael as soon as possible.

While Michael waited for an appointment, he sought out various individuals within the fort and learned that Captain McGillycuddy had worked with other Indian agents at other frontier forts. Captain McGillycuddy was a highly regarded medical surgeon and had been recommended for his present position as Indian agent by his close friend John Dougherty. Dougherty was in charge of the entire Upper Missouri Agency for the Department of Indian Affairs and considered highly experienced as a roving ambassador and one who conscientiously strived to maintain peace and obtain Indian lands in nonviolent ways.

Some agents did their jobs honorably amid the terrible living conditions that prevailed on the reservations and reserves. Others were convinced that the only way the Native peoples could survive was by becoming individualized Christian farmers who made a living on their own pieces of private property. Still others were corrupt, taking advantage of the remoteness of their situations by skimming their charges' annuities or by colluding with settlers to steal Indian lands. Michael wondered which category Captain McGillycuddy fit into.

Philomene found time away from her duties at the hospital to discuss Michael's plight with the captain and requested that the captain meet with her husband. After hearing Philomene's plea, Captain McGillycuddy seemed eager to discuss possibilities with Michael. He set an appointment for the next evening after duties were completed.

Michael was elated with this news and began preparing his thoughts for an in-depth discussion with the captain. The particular area he felt he could build on was the area of the basic duties of an Indian agent that suggested maintaining flexible cooperation with U.S. Army military personnel. Second, he wished to discuss the true reasons for his interest, which stemmed back to his leaving his home in Germany and the persecution he had experienced because of his activities with the Freedom Fighters. Michael intended to stress the obvious similarities between the Indians and the U.S. government.

The meeting went far better than Michael had hoped. Michael and Captain McGillycuddy were in close harmony on every issue they discussed. He was delighted when the captain suggested that he would follow up with Michael's commanding officers concerning some sort of transfer to Indian Affairs.

Michael returned to Philomene late that evening, surprised and thrilled by his presentation and discussion with the captain. He spent the next few days in a state of controlled excitement. When he finally received the order to report immediately to the colonel's headquarters, he nearly exploded with anticipation.

The colonel, well aware of Michael's past service and the fact that only a few months remained of his enlistment, agreed to an immediate transfer of Michael to serve under Captain McGillycuddy as an Indian agent. With this announcement, as a man restless for fresh horizons, Michael emitted a huge sigh of relief.

CHAPTER 44
LEARNING INDIAN CULTURE

With this new assignment, Michael and Philomene had to leave their current accommodations and take up residence closer to the hospital and to Captain McGillycuddy in his new capacity. The second thing Michael had to do was obtain civilian clothing at the fort's trading post. The new clothing was necessary so the Indian tribes, with whom they would come in contact, would recognize them as friendlier than they would if they were dressed in military uniform. The blue soldier uniforms were dreaded, even hated, by most Indians because of the soldiers' past deeds. Michael was happy to learn that the government would pick up the tab for this necessary clothing.

On returning home, Michael immediately dressed in his new civilian clothing and presented himself to Philomene in the next room. As he entered the room, Philomene gasped in admiration. This was the first time she had seen him dressed in anything other than his uniform. With the civilian clothes came the revelation of what the future had in store for them.

Wearing his new clothing, Michael met Captain McGillycuddy at a facility outside the fort. This meeting was to discuss the immediate actions to be taken and to meet the interpreter that Captain McGillycuddy had employed to complete their small team of Indian agent activists.

Michael took an immediate liking to Chaytan, the Indian interpreter, and learned why he had been chosen by the captain for this particular job. Chaytan was a Lakota Sioux whose name meant "falcon" or "hawk" in Lakota. A great name, Michael thought, for this rather tall impressive Indian with his massive chest and arms that denoted strength, power, and muscular endurance.

The three spoke for hours about how the Indians and the white pioneers were caught in a web of their own weaving and how hatred on each side had evolved. They further contemplated the importance of actions necessary to counteract some of these feelings, a difficult task that would require alertness and a great deal of patience and understanding of both sides of the problem.

The captain declared that in a couple of days, they would venture outside the fort to make their first contact with an Indian tribe that had a particular complaint with some of the soldiers of the fort. In preparation for this contact, Michael was to retrieve forty-two sacred eagle feathers that had been wrongfully seized from the tribe by a sergeant of that outfit.

CHAPTER 45
INTO THE UNKNOWN

Armed with a letter from the captain, written on Indian Agency stationary, Michael approached the headquarters of the particular outfit. It wasn't easy to reach the commanding officer, but finally his persistence paid off and he was ushered into the headquarters. After saluting, Michael presented the commanding officer with the letter.

On good authority, the letter accused a particular sergeant of unlawfully seizing forty-two sacred feathers. It further suggested the ramifications of not immediately returning them to the Indian tribe to whom they belonged.

The commanding officer sent for the sergeant in question, ordering him to report to headquarters immediately and bring with him the feathers that he had appropriated.

Shortly the sergeant appeared, but he had only some of the feathers with him. On questioning, the sergeant admitted he had traded some of the feathers to other soldiers for souvenirs. Hearing this, the commanding officer ordered the sergeant to return to his outfit, retrieve all of the feathers, and report back to headquarters within the hour. He further threatened to put the sergeant in the guardhouse if this order was not acted on completely and immediately.

On his way out the door, the sergeant gave Michael a look that could not be mistaken for anything other than pure animosity.

Within the hour, and with all forty-two feathers in hand, Michael began his withdrawal. He immediately encountered a large gathering of soldiers of the sergeant's outfit blocking his passage. All Michael's inner warning systems went off at once. With a quick intake of breath like someone about to plunge into icy water, he began pushing his way through the gathering, ignoring the dirty looks, the cursing, the tobacco juice spit on his boots, and the fists shaking in his face. As he reached safety, he promised himself to avoid future interactions with this particular outfit.

Captain McGillycuddy commended Michael on his promptness and his achievement. He recognized that this had not been an easy task for him.

The captain, Michael, and the Indian translator Chaytan met for the last time before their trip into Indian country. They agreed that nothing they took with them must, in any way, connect them to the military. Even the horses and the saddles and saddle blankets must be carefully selected. Captain McGillycuddy was to be referred to by his first name only: Val, for Valentine, and Private Michael Myers as simply Michael. At the conclusion of this meeting, the forty-two feathers were carefully placed in a special box to protect them from damage on their perilous journey. Shortly after the crack of dawn, dressed in their civilian clothing, the three set off into the unknown.

CHAPTER 46
CONTACTING THE TRIBE

Chaytan had spoken with other Indian scouts and interpreters to determine which tribe these feathers belonged to. He had also learned the approximate location where the tribe might now be found. This was very helpful information, and they set off in the direction so indicated.

On the second or third day out, they became aware that they were being watched and hoped that the presence of Chaytan would guarantee their safe passage farther into the valley.

As they made camp that night, Chaytan let Val and Michael know, in low tones, that they were surrounded and they must do nothing that might make matters worse. Sleep was difficult to attain that night, especially for Val and Michael.

Early the next morning, Chaytan went to the nearby creek to fill their canteens and was quickly surrounded by three of the Indians he knew had been watching their camp. He greeted them in their native tongue and explained they had come in peace and were seeking a powwow with their chief. He then asked them to accompany him back to the campsite.

As they approached the campsite, the remaining Indians who had surrounded the campsite during the night came into full view. When Val and Michael offered them food and drink, they relaxed and came closer. At the request of Val, Chaytan asked if their village was nearby and if they would take the white men to meet with their chief. After a brief exchange among themselves, the Indians agreed to take Val and Michael, with Chaytan acting as their interpreter, for a powwow with their chief.

On entering the village, Val and Michael noticed that it was not alive with action. The few Indians they observed outside the teepees moved slowly and did not seem at all concerned about the strangers now entering. Chaytan became immediately concerned and told the captain that something was not normal in this village and that he suspected some sickness had befallen its inhabitants. Their meeting with the chieftain confirmed that a sickness had fallen on his village.

After examining one of the sick Indians, Dr. McGillycuddy knew immediately that a smallpox epidemic had infiltrated the tribe. Through his interpreter, he learned that this invisible killer had been brought to the village recently by white traders. It was common practice that such traders would trade blankets for buffalo skins. In this case, the traded blankets were infected with smallpox.

Captain McGillycuddy recalled a memorandum that he had seen on his appointment as Indian agent that confirmed such practice as an approved practice. Years earlier, Colonel Henry Bouquet, at Fort Pitt, had recommended inoculating the Indians with smallpox by means of blankets, as well as every other method possible that could serve to exterminate the race.

Such practice had been employed for some time in the Minnesota wilderness, and Michael began to believe some of the rumors that he had previously heard, including that more Indians died of various white man diseases than in warfare.

It was beyond Michael's comprehension that the U.S.

government believed the Indian problem could be solved by force and purposeful extinction. Both Michael and Dr. McGillycuddy felt sickened by this reality.

The tribe inhabiting this village was not the tribe they sought to return the forty-two sacred feathers to, and so they prepared to leave the village. Dr. McGillycuddy insisted to the chief that all traded blankets and related items immediately be put to flame. New blankets would be sent to replace those burned, and the blankets would be delivered to them by wagon within the next two weeks. McGillycuddy gave his word, and the chief thanked him.

The tribe that McGillycuddy, Michael, and Chaytan were seeking lived a half day's ride farther to the north. The chief offered a couple of his braves to escort them, but Dr. McGillycuddy declined and suggested that all braves remain in their native village until the sickness had completely passed. The chief, however, had different thoughts. He told them he would feel honored if two of his braves could accompany them to ensure their safe arrival at the intended village. He would order the braves not to enter the village but to return home before doing so. It was so agreed.

The next morning as the group prepared to leave, the chief spoke a word that sounded like "Chick a son" to both McGillycuddy and Michael and gave the sign that corresponded to the spoken word. The chief touched the center of his chest with his left hand and waved his hand toward the group with his palm up. Chaytan translated the word and action as meaning "Friends." The last word spoken by the chief, "Kataka ab," was translated as "Hostility flown."

As they rode toward this next destination, McGillycuddy and Michael agreed they had learned a great deal about Indian relationships and hoped to learn even more on reaching their ultimate goal of returning the forty-two sacred feathers. Only time would tell.

CHAPTER 47

THE SACRED FEATHERS

The braves knew the location of the neighboring tribe and guided them within sight of the village. As they turned to return to their own village, Michael gave them a smile and made the sign that meant "Friend." One brave immediately returned Michael's gesture, along with a smile. Very unusual for Indians, both Michael and McGillycuddy thought. Another lesson learned.

As the two Indians who had accompanied them disappeared in the distance, two Indians from the new village approached them. Apparently they had been watching the group for some time. Chaytan said, "These white men wish to speak with your chief concerning an important matter." The Indians understood and motioned them to the village.

Their initial meeting with the chief went smoothly. They learned this tribe had been physically removed from Iowa Territory and were on their way to a nearby reservation. They further learned that on their travels a few moons ago, they had been attacked by blue jackets soldiers wishing to lighten their load so they could move more rapidly to their new location. The blue jackets soldiers had searched their travois and helped themselves to a lot of the Indians' belongings. This explained how the sacred feathers had been obtained by the sergeant.

The chief explained that the absence of these sacred feathers further hindered their journey to the reservation. Hearing this, on a wink from McGillycuddy's right eye, Michael departed the tepee to retrieve the package of feathers from McGillycuddy's horse.

The chief could not believe his good fortune as he opened the package and discovered all forty-two feathers. He immediately ran out of the tepee and through the village waving them above his head and proclaiming his joy for their return.

A celebration, best described as one of happiness and joy, was held that evening around a huge bonfire. As the evening celebration came to a close, McGillycuddy, Michael, and their Lakota Sioux Indian guide, Chaytan, were each pulled into the tribe's closing dance of thanksgiving. Michael felt humbled by the honor.

Like before, two braves were assigned to them by the chief, to guarantee their safe journey home. The entire village showed up to send them on their way. The Indians' voices were high pitched, crisp, and clear. In the chilly morning air, Michael welcomed those voices like a warm embrace. The voices echoed until Michael's group was over the hill and out of sight.

As they continued their ride back to the fort, Michael and McGillycuddy had a great deal of time to discuss the adventure they just concluded. They committed to continue their efforts in championing the cause of the Native Americans. Easier said than done!

CHAPTER 48
UNEASINESS

Philomene was relieved when Michael arrived home safely and was eager to hear about his latest adventure. As Michael related his experience, Philomene marveled at the bravery of the trio that had ventured into Indian territory without the U.S. Army's protection. Michael assured her that the army, or the "blue pants" as the Indians called them, would have created a much larger problem had they been along.

Michael's first order of business was to take the order from Captain McGillycuddy to the quartermaster, so that new blankets would be promptly delivered to the Indians as promised. The blankets would be charged to the Indian agent's account. Michael assured the quartermaster that McGillycuddy would be checking to make sure the delivery was made and further offered the services of Chaytan to guide them to the village if necessary.

Having gained confidence from this last episode with Indian tribes, McGillycuddy, Michael, and Chaytan ventured out, during the next few months, to meet with other Indian tribes to determine their moods and needs. McGillycuddy recognized that Michael's time in the army was quickly drawing to a close and wished to take full advantage of their successes before he was mustered out.

As Michael and Philomene counted the days remaining for his service to the army, they felt a creeping uneasiness about entering into civilian life. At dinner each night they discussed various possibilities. The days passed with nervous frustration.

This frustration was recognized by Captain McGillycuddy, who knew Michael as a man restless for fresh horizons. He sat down with Michael and suggested a possible solution to the frustration the couple was now experiencing.

The captain had recently heard from the Indian agent at Fort Clark that a town named Peoria in Illinois Territory had grown up around the fort and now had a population of almost 2,000 people. The old fort was currently being rebuilt by the Peoria residents as further protection against the Black Hawk Indians. Although the recent Black Hawk wars were now a thing of the past, they wanted the comfort and safety of the fort, which they believed would solidify the town's future. The captain suggested that Michael and Philomene consider this place among their options of where they would settle.

Although communication was slow and somewhat incomplete, they did learn that the townspeople had recently voted that the little town of Peoria, Illinois should become a city. One of the first actions that the new mayor, William Hale, had taken was to ensure the landing area for the steamships was adequate and necessary for Peoria to grow and be at the center of new activity.

Further investigation confirmed that steamship travel down the Mississippi and up the Illinois River would get travelers to Peoria with little travel by wagon. Should travelers wish to go farther, steamship travel was readily available to St. Louis and all the way down to New Orleans.

Michael sat quietly, turning over in his mind what they had just learned. Philomene was in the far corner of the room but watched carefully as Michael further considered their future.

Shortly, Michael smiled in her direction, and as she smiled back he jumped to his feet, ran across the room, grabbed her at the waist with both hands, and swung her around the room. It was obvious that Michael had found all of his emotions agreeable. Peoria it was! Philomene executed a playful pirouette to show her agreement.

CHAPTER 49
NEW CIVILIAN LIFE

The day finally arrived and Michael was mustered out of his service to the U.S. Army by 12 noon. The evening was devoted to celebration, partying, and farewell good-byes.

The next morning he received his final pay and a government script for one horse. This was common practice for frontier soldiers to aid them on their way back to civilization.

Michael and Philomene's financial situation was good due to the savings they had made along the way. They were able to purchase a surplus wagon from the quartermaster sergeant for the nominal price of $40. On its receipt Michael inspected it carefully to make sure it was safe for traveling, and he repacked all the bearings of the wooden wheels.

Before the close of the week, they loaded their wagon with their few belongings and were off to Fort Snelling on the Mississippi River to board the paddle boat for their trip to Peoria.

The trip down the Mississippi and up the Illinois River to Peoria was without incident. On arrival, Michael and Philomene found time to explore this visibly soul-stifling town. Comparing notes in the evening, they both felt that they had stepped into an entirely different world. The town was a boring place with a dismal population. It seemed to them that the town was a mixture of the quaint, the spectacular, and the tacky. This was not the town they had expected.

The fact that this town was not what they had hoped for became abundantly clear when one of the friends they had made along the journey lay beaten senseless, robbed, and left for dead. He died 9 days later. But during his lucid moments, the man gave a good description of the three men who had attacked him.

A huge posse was formed and out they went. Shortly the three men were captured and brought back to town. News that the posse had captured and not immediately hung the culprits was indeed surprising to the townspeople. When a rumor started in town that the hanging would be postponed, a mob stormed the courthouse demanding that the killers be turned over to them for justice. The sheriff and the deputies fought the rioters, injuring two and killing one man.

The men were sentenced to hang on January 15, 1851. It was a damned blustery frigid day as folk began to gather at the gallows constructed out in the town square. The crowd of 3,000 people roared, as the wagon containing the condemned men rolled inside a fenced area. As the terrified men were seized from the wagon and paraded up the gallows steps, the crowd surged forward knocking the surrounding fence flat to the ground.

Once up on the platform, the two men turned to face the sea of angry faces. The noise began to lessen and soon the crowd stood silently looking up at the condemned men. The hangman guided a black hood over each killer's head and as the padre mumbled prayers, the snap of the opening trapdoor rang out in the cold morning air, hurdling the men to their deaths. A mighty roar went up and then silence as the bodies began to twist slowly at the end of the ropes. This was the first public hanging in the city of Peoria and far too much for Michael and Philomene to wipe from their minds. They did not care to live among people who considered public hangings as entertainment.

This spectacle, coupled with the area's support for slavery, convinced Michael and Philomene that their opportunities were definitely to be found elsewhere.

CHAPTER 50
THE ST. LOUIS ADVENTURE

Michael learned that great numbers of emigrants from Ireland and Germany were now arriving in St. Louis. The population had grown in the previous 10 years from less than 20,000 people to almost 75,000 people in the year 1850. St. Louis now had a greater population than New Orleans, where Philomene was born. This was largely due to its busy port and train connections. Given the city's proximity to the free state of Illinois, it attracted slaves escaping to freedom where they found work in the many jobs on the waterfront as well as on the riverboats.

The additional fact that St. Louis was becoming a main gateway to the West helped convince Michael and Philomene that new opportunities could be found there for a couple seeking freedom from a barbaric civilization. These opportunities also seemed to fit with Michael's continual restlessness for fresh horizons.

On their way downriver, troubling news reached them of a disaster that had befallen St. Louis. On average, five steamboats arrived each day and their landing on the levee caused great plumes of smoke to fill the skies above. Some of these steamboats were 300 feet long. One of the paddle wheel steamboats had caught fire while secured to the levee, and soon the ship's moorings had burned through. The boat floated down the levee, crashing into nearby steamers and eventually spreading the fire to twenty-three other boats. The fire then jumped to land and soon engulfed huge piles of freight on the levee and continued to spread to the nearby buildings. The great fire engulfed more than 400 buildings and left the levee in total chaos. On their arrival, Philomene and Michael found the massive devastation was far worse than they had expected.

While St. Louis reeled from the fire's destruction, new concerns struck the city in the form of a cholera epidemic. In addition, another bacterial infection, carried by new immigrants from Germany and Holland as they traveled up the Mississippi River from New Orleans to St. Louis, plagued the population.

The combined cholera epidemic and bacterial infection disseminated the north and south sides of the city and killed almost 5,000 residents, about 6% of the city's total population. The epidemic brought to Philomene's mind her own youth and the loss of her parents in a similar epidemic in New Orleans.

Consequently, Michael and Philomene settled on the outskirts of the city and stayed to themselves as much as possible. Michael sought employment outside the city. He wanted to be nowhere near the levee and its devastation and health problems.

Their adjustment to civilian life did not come easy. St. Louis was filled with lots of people, curious sounds, and unusual smells. Again, they felt as if they had stepped into another world. However, the idea slowly germinated within them to settle in the city, as they patiently explored their options for the future.

Michael found employment at the local livery, and Philomene was soon being called on frequently for her expertise as a midwife. This brought them in touch with many people moving farther west into the unknown.

In addition to Michael's duties at the local livery, selling horses and oxen to the pioneers moving farther west, he became an all-around handy man and knowledgeable as a wheelwright. Philomene became occupied with their three daughters, Caroline, born in 1853, with Margaret and Mollie following shortly thereafter.

After almost 10 years in St. Louis, Michael began to feel society closing in on him and his family. The city had grown considerably and even though they had chosen to live just outside the city, they found themselves now surrounded by thousands of neighbors.

Michael grew excited hearing from returning wagon masters about the freedom and open spaces of the frontier farther west. He began dreaming of new opportunities to breathe freely again and to join the adventures of this growing frontier.

CHAPTER 51
PREPARING TO LEAVE

Early in 1859, news reached St. Louis that in the fall of 1858, gold had been discovered in Ralston Creek in Auraria, Colorado Territory, just southwest of Denver City. This news sparked the Pike's Peak Gold Rush.

Although Michael was not particularly interested in the search for gold, he saw it as a unique opportunity for profits in other areas and further discussed this with Philomene. It did not take much discussion before it was agreed to leave St. Louis as soon as such a move could be made.

Michael immediately went to work on the old "honeymoon" covered wagon he had lovingly maintained over the years. It needed only a couple of repairs and some updating to be ready for the long, arduous journey across the prairie.

Recognizing that they would be traveling through Indian country, Michael sought out Russell Green, the most experienced wagon master, to lead the families on a successful and safe journey. Because of numerous previous dealings with Russell Green, Michael had no problem reserving travel on the next wagon train traveling to Colorado Territory.

Though prices and availability of goods necessary for the trip varied from year to year, most emigrants discovered it cost a minimum of $600 to $800 to assemble the basics required: a wagon, oxen, and supplies. The old "honeymoon" schooner was to prove worthy of the approximately 750-mile trip and the 3 months it would take to make the journey to Denver City. Michael, again, felt rewarded for preserving this old treasure. The purchase or trading for the necessary oxen was another matter, but having been in the business for many years, Michael experienced no particular problem with this task.

Some emigrants preferred horses or mules to pull their wagons, but Michael learned that for the route they were to take, oxen would serve them better. Although oxen were slower, walking only 2 or 3 miles an hour, they could more easily pull a lot of weight, survive on little food, and were patient, gentle, and easy to train. They were also less expensive than horses or mules and would be more useful to pull a plow later, if necessary.

Philomene busied herself with making a list and gathering the items needed to survive the long trip. Whatever they included must be kept below 2,000 pounds in total weight. It was generally known that a greater weight would tire the animals, and many pioneers would have to discard excess food or other items along the way.

Philomene's list consisted of minimal cooking utensils, including a cast iron skillet, Dutch oven, reflector oven, coffee pot, tin plates, cups, knives, forks, spoons, matches, crocks, canteens, buckets, and water bags. Additional items included a rifle, pistol, lead and shot for hunting along the way and for self-defense, candles for light (rather than transporting lanterns and oil, which were heavy), and several pounds of soap. Basic tools such as a shovel, ax, and tools to repair the wagon if necessary were also on the list. They would take only two or three sets of practical, sturdy, warm clothing made of wool and linen, a small sewing kit to mend clothes as needed, and some towels and rags for personal hygiene. Bedding and tents completed the list of necessities, leaving little space for other items.

However, a few toys were added to help their three daughters pass the time.

When the list was shown to Michael, he gave a hardy laugh and pointed out that she had overlooked items of great importance. Michael suggested a quick visit with Russell Green, the wagon master.

The wagon master complimented Philomene on her list and mentioned that he had just sent out notices to all those who had signed up for the trip to attend a special meeting. At that meeting he would discuss the trip in more detail. At Philomene's begging for advance information, the wagon master gave her his food supply recommendations for a typical family of four: 800 pounds of flour, 200 pounds of lard, 700 pounds of bacon, 200 pounds of beans, 100 pounds of fruit, 75 pounds of coffee and 25 pounds of salt, and don't forget pepper and saleratus for baking and, of course, water barrels for storing much-needed water along the way. He also suggested whiskey, brandy, and medicines.

At the wagon master's special meeting, after he had told the travelers about the requirements necessary to take with them, he discussed the route they would be taking and the hazards that they could expect along the way.

Even though the Indian tribes had been peaceful in recent months, travel along this route was hazardous because of lack of water and game. The only source of water was from sparse springs and a few ephemeral waterholes and streams along the way.

The wagon master estimated that some of the people making the trip would die along the route. "Cholera," he told them, "is a bacterial disease that causes severe diarrhea and vomiting and you can die from it. Most victims die from dehydration within hours of contracting the disease." He added that poor sanitary conditions should be avoided at all costs.

The other leading causes of death along the way, he continued, would be from accidents with wagons, firearms, and drowning at river crossings. This trip would require several treacherous river crossings and emigrants who were not experienced in handling wagons or coping with runaway livestock could have serious problems.

He further cautioned that fatigue from the rigors of daily travel, poor nutrition, typhoid, or food poisoning may claim others. He suggested anyone nervous or fearful after hearing these stories might wish to reconsider taking the journey. In closing he told them, "The wagon train leaves one week from today!"

CHAPTER 52
OFF TO KANSAS TERRITORY

Only twenty-two of the previously expected twenty-four wagons showed up on the morning of departure. Apparently, two of the wagons had decided to cancel the trip after hearing the wagon master's comments about the possible dangers. Philomene and Michael were assigned the position of the third wagon in the procession. This was welcome news since they would not be eating dust as they would if their position were farther back in the train.

The wagon master gathered all the members of the train and described his expectations for this first day of travel. Because they were getting a late start, the distance to be traveled would be shorter than what would be required after this first day. Periodic short stops would be made each day to address nature's calls: men were to go to the right of the train and women to the left. Additionally, stops for lunch each day would be made at the wagon master's discretion so that the animals could rest in areas where food and water might be found. Any problems, disagreements, or concerns should be brought to the wagon master's attention immediately, as he would act as judge and jury, having the final say on everything.

The wagons formed up and the command of "Wagons Ho!" was given and off they went on their yet unknown adventure.

The first leg of their journey from St. Louis to Independence, Missouri presented no major problems. The 25 days it had taken to cover the 240 miles, over relatively level terrain, provided a great deal of the experience necessary for the more treacherous portions of their trip yet to come.

After a day's rest and replenishing their supplies in Independence, the wagon train was off on the hundred-mile trip to Trail Junction, the junction of the Santa Fe Trail and the Smoky Hill Trail. Many of the travelers thought the name Smoky Hill was so named because of Indians and their smoke signals along the way. This misunderstanding was quickly corrected by the wagon master, who told them that farther along the trail they would see that the name came from the hazy smoke that often surrounded the river and landmark buttes. His explanation calmed some of the travelers' fears.

The explanation was short-lived when they heard that a previous train, led by the Blue brothers, got caught in a desolate area. When one of the members died, the surviving members were forced into cannibalism. Again, the wagon master assured them that although the trail was far harder and more dangerous than other prairie trails to the Rockies, the possibility of an Indian attack was scarce and that the traveling, at this time of year, was the best time to avoid similar problems. Their main problem would be the scarcity of water, wild game, and grazing for their animals.

The first casualty happened a few days later. A 7-year-old girl, tired of walking beside the wagon, attempted to jump up on the wagon while it was moving rather than waiting for the wagon to stop for a nature break. She slipped and fell under the wagon and was by crushed by the back wheels. She died instantly.

The train came to a halt while the pioneers held services and buried her on the trail. The wagon master suggested this site as the best place for the burial since it would not be disturbed by wild animals. Wagons passing along the trail would compact the recently disturbed earth, thus protecting the gravesite.

The second casualty happened when the wagon train was crossing their first river. Each wagon was to follow the wagon in front of it closely for safety reasons. Wagon number 15 lost control of his horses when they became fearful of the rising water and faster current. The horses bolted, pulling the wagon into deeper water and causing it to overturn and be swept away. Both husband and wife were lost, along with their wagon and all their possessions. They were buried on the hillside overlooking the site where the tragedy had occurred.

These tragic events lay heavy on the minds and actions of all members of the wagon train and made them wonder what other dangers lay in wait for them.

CHAPTER 53
LURKING DISEASES AND ILLNESSES

As the train continued moving west along Smoky Hill Trail, a new hazard became a reality – the lack of water and game. Some on the wagon train had not heeded the wagon master's caution concerning their use of water and conserving as much as possible between waterholes. The wagons were now down to less than 2 days of drinking water and no extra water for their animals.

In the past few weeks, the dry grass that normally surrounded these areas, used by travelers for their animals, had disappeared completely. Consequently, many of the travelers and their animals were now suffering from thirst or starvation. Many of the better prepared travelers, reluctantly, shared some of their water and dry food supplies with others in need. Fear for their own safety limited this generosity to a very short period of time.

By the first of June, the animals either became too weak to pull the wagons or died trying. The number of animal deaths increased daily, and these were followed by many human deaths, further slowing the advance of the wagon train toward the next watering hole. Soon, the pioneers found no more game along the route, so they resorted to butchering and drying the meat of the fallen oxen.

Cholera and other illnesses became frequent, unstoppable passengers as the wagon train continued farther west.

When the wagon train reached the chalk bluffs in Kansas Territory, the pioneers knew that they had completed approximately two thirds of their travel to Denver. The Smoky Hill River they followed was dry. As they stopped for the night, the wagon master suggested they dig down a few feet in the dry river bed to see if they could tap into some water.

After a meager dinner, the men and women dug feverishly toward their salvation in the ground. Luckily, at two feet down, their efforts were rewarded. Water barrels were refilled and long exhalations of relief were heard throughout the encampment. An extra day was spent enjoying their thirst-quenching discovery.

CHAPTER 54
CLOSING IN ON DENVER CITY

The wagon train paused briefly at a fork in the trail where Fort Wallace was under construction. The South Fork would take travelers 200 miles to Fort Wise and the connection to the Santa Fe Trail. Within a day's travel, the other fork would take them farther into Kansas Territory.

The wagon master rode the length of the train to announce that they were now in Kansas Territory and approximately only 30 days from their final destination, Denver City/Auraria, Kansas Territory. As he passed each wagon, cheers rang out indicating a celebration of some sort was in order.

As the sun began to sink beyond the western horizon, the celebration was in full swing. Shortly, the celebration was interrupted, as one of the outpost scouts rode into the camp to report Indians had been sighted on the low rising hills to the north.

The celebrating travelers felt a sudden chill, as if cold water had been poured onto them. Glances were exchanged as a creeping uneasiness began to build in the bottom of their hearts. The scout's announcement infected the remaining hours of the evening, and most travelers carried the thoughts of tomorrow into restless sleep.

Not so for Michael. He immediately sought out the wagon master for his thoughts on the report. Michael learned that in this particular area there were at least four Indian tribes: the Arapahoe, Cheyenne, Kiowa, and possibly some Sioux and Utes. Of these tribes, the Cheyenne and Sioux were most warlike. Few problems had been reported with the Arapahoe, Ute, or Kiowa tribes.

Michael briefed the wagon master concerning his past activities with the Indians and offered any help that he might provide should it become necessary. Michael and Philomene slept soundly.

The next morning the wagon train moved farther west toward Denver and intersected with two other trails. One trail went south from the Oregon/Overland Trail to Fort Wise and the Santa Fe Trail, and the other, the Republican

Fork Trail, came from the northeast and joined the Smoky Hill Trail at Big Sandy Creek. No Indians were sighted until the wagon train started moving along the North Smoky Hill Trail toward Kiowa and the Cutoff Road to Denver City.

There, the pioneers sighted five Indians sitting on horses atop the low rising hill a short distance from the trail. The wagon master arrived at Michael and Philomene's wagon with an extra saddle horse and asked Michael to accompany him to the head of the wagon train. Without hesitation, Michael was in the saddle riding alongside the wagon master.

As the wagon train approached the hill where the Indians had gathered, the order was given to halt. Michael removed his gun belt holding his six-shooter and handed it to the driver of the first wagon and suggested the wagon master do likewise with both his pistol and his rifle. The two unarmed men rode slowly toward the stationary Indians. The occupants of the wagon train breathlessly watched the action unfold.

As they came closer to the Indians, Michael raised his hand

and arm to signal the Indian greeting and friendship sign that he had previously learned. He hoped his hard swallow had gone undetected by the Indians and had not betrayed his nervousness that the signal may not be recognized. When he and the wagon master were within 10 feet of the Indians, the greeting he had given was returned by the apparent leader of the group.

Through sign language, Michael learned that they were hungry and wished to trade with the wagon train for food for their families. The wagon master agreed and Michael and he, followed by the Indians, made their way down to the wagon train.

After word spread among the wagon train about the plight of the Indians and their requirement for food for their families, the pioneers were more than generous and required little of trade goods in return. This experience brought home to Michael and others of the wagon train the effect that the white man was having on the Indians.

CHAPTER 55

THREE DAYS TO DENVER CITY

The wagon train observed small groups of Indians on horses next to the trail, but this was not as unsettling as their first experience. They realized the Indians wanted to trade for food. The more they stopped to trade, the faster their stock of food items became depleted. It was as if word had spread of their willingness to share their dwindling supply of food the closer they got to their final destination.

Soon they entered a small valley surrounded by pine trees, where both water and grassland were available. Except for a number of Indian braves on the bluffs above the valley, this was the perfect place for their evening stop. The Indians just sat there observing the wagon train rather than coming down to trade. They seemed different than the other groups of Indians the pioneers had encountered. Consequently, the wagon master, to guard against problems, increased the number of armed men watching the cattle and horses.

Though the night passed peaceably, in the morning the Indians struck. One group went after the cattle, attacking the guards, while the second group went toward the wagons, screeching like demons and beating dry deerskin to stampede the stock.

It was an uneven contest. The Indians were armed only with bows and arrows and a few old inaccurate rifles while the defenders had much newer rifles and knew how to use them. In about 10 minutes the Indians retreated, leaving behind thirty of their dead and wounded. The wagon train lost two men, and two others were wounded.

In the full light of day, they discovered some of their horses missing. They followed the trail of the robbers and by evening they found the thieving Indians, thought to be Utes, sleeping by a campfire. The men recovered their horses and returned to the wagon train to resume their journey.

Without any further incidents with the Indians, the wagon train stopped briefly to water their animals at the construction site for the Kiowa stage station. In the afternoon they passed the Parker 17 Mile House and knew then that they would be at their final destination the very next day.

No one could say that the journey had been an easy one. Of the twenty-two wagons that had started out, only sixteen completed the journey. Of the original eighty individuals, fifteen had been tragically lost, and five remained incapacitated with broken bones, gunshot wounds, or other unknown sicknesses. Because of Michael and Philomene's close attention during this journey, their three young daughters remained healthy, happy, and eager for new adventures.

CHAPTER 56
DENVER CITY, JULY 1859

It was somewhat confusing as the wagon train entered the outskirts of the city. Some signage referred to it as Denver City, some as Auraria, and still a third referenced it as St. Charles. It really didn't make much of a difference. They knew they had reached their final destination where two rivers met to form one larger river.

As they checked into the "Elephant Corral," to leave their animals to be cared for and fed, they learned that all three names for the city were correct. The names referred to settlements on various sides of the river. However, the name Denver had been suggested for the entire area in hopes of gaining political favor since it would be named after the Kansas territorial governor, James Denver. This did not sit well with everyone.

The name "Elephant Corral" was so unusual it caught the curiosity of Philomene and Michael and their daughters. They learned the name was probably associated with the perilous crossing of the continent, when "seeing the elephant" became synonymous with seeing something strange, wonderful, and perhaps a little frightening. Here, it was where emigrants watered, boarded, fed, and traded livestock.

The city that now lined the banks of the South Platte River consisted of tents, teepees, wagons, lean-tos, and crudely constructed log cabins that were inhabited by prospectors and fortune seekers. Gold was the main attraction. Mining camps served both as a landmark and a rallying cry for weary travelers. The "Pikes Peak or Bust" gold rush was in full force.

Gold wasn't the only way to strike it rich in the boomtown that was springing up. Early arrivers simply staked out a claim to the land, laid out city streets, and sold lots to the new arrivals.

By the fall of 1859, the situation on both sides of the South Platte was tenuous and chaotic. Tensions between the cities grew. The newly established *Rocky Mountain News* ran an article describing the metropolis as a "log city of 150 dwellings, not three-fourths completed nor two-thirds inhabited, nor one-third fit to be." Finally, a torch-lit meeting was held, and on the one bridge over Cherry Creek, for the price of a barrel of whiskey, all other names were dropped and the settlement united as one under the name "Denver."

Philomene and Michael quickly discovered that housing conditions were appalling, even for those used to frontier living. They found hundreds of families living in wagons, tents, and shelters made of carpets and bedding. Since Michael and Philomene's funds were almost exhausted, they had no alternative but to find an open area by the river and join other families who were living in their wagons.

When Michael heard that a blacksmith could make $8 to $10 a day, he drew on his past experiences and applied for employment at the Elephant Corral. When he related these experiences, he was quickly offered a job. Because they already had a blacksmith, he would be the blacksmith's assistant and would not earn anywhere near the amount he had heard. Adding his experience in the army with animals and the number of years working at a livery stable in St. Louis helped him add to his earnings. This would satisfy him for the time being.

Philomene set up a soup kitchen by the river, not far from their wagon, which proved to be an immediate success with the numerous fortune seekers arriving daily. Equipment was scarce and primitive. Her hours were long and, in some regards, reminded her of her time as an indentured servant. However, now she was doing this for her own family and with free will. Staying near their wagon and her growing daughters added everyday enjoyment to this otherwise tedious work.

As Philomene and Michael's life became somewhat settled, a huge gold strike was discovered in the Rocky Mountain town of Central City. As quickly as they came to Denver, fortune seekers packed and headed to the hills, leaving the city nearly deserted.

CHAPTER 57
THE WILL TO SURVIVE AND THRIVE

Gradually, people returned to Denver as they battled harsh weather conditions in the mountains. They figured they were better off seeking their fortune in the city than to keep searching for gold that may never materialize. They discovered and enjoyed the mild, year-round climate that Denver offered, and the city was establishing itself as a trade center.

The *Rocky Mountain News* helped the growth of the city by publishing an article highlighting Denver as a fascinating place to live. The article stated, "Denver is such an unlikely place for a city to be. It began as a little town in the middle of nowhere, with no obvious reason to be there. It was as if angels had carried a city to a proper place and accidentally dropped it here."

Denver in 1860, with approximately 2,000 inhabitants, was not a sure thing. Similar to other mining towns, it could easily die and become a ghost town. Michael and Philomene were happy with the size of the city. They particularly liked the open spaces, the sky, and the freedom that it offered them and their small family.

Michael, not interested in searching for gold, continued with his employment at the Elephant Corral while Philomene continued with her soup kitchen. A small school had been started in the upper floor of one of the numerous saloons. Schooling hours were to be from 9 a.m. until 1 p.m., 5 days a week. Neither Philomene nor Michael had much formal education but recognized the importance it would have for their children's future. All three were enrolled, since the cost was rather small and the family budget could now afford it.

Philomene took advantage of the extra free time the schooling provided for her duties with her soup kitchen. She began feeding lunch to nearly twenty men daily.

During the next year, prospectors and fortune seekers continued to come to the area. They came from all over the country, traveling on foot, by covered wagons, by horseback, and even pushing their belongings in wheelbarrows. In 1860 the United States was a divided nation that had eighteen free states and fifteen slave states. Battle lines were drawn. On February 28, 1861, Denver City, Kansas Territory became Denver, Colorado Territory, by proclamation of U.S. President James Buchanan. On April 13, 1861, the *Rocky Mountain News* reported that Confederate forces had fired on Fort Sumter and war had been declared in retaliation.

Abraham Lincoln appointed William Gilpin governor of the new Colorado Territory. On his arrival in Denver, Gilpin found the new territory had only two disbanded companies of volunteers to keep peace between the whites and the Indians and the ever-increasing animosity between the Confederacy and the Union sympathizers.

Not only was it necessary to keep the peace between the whites and Indians but between the many different tribes that inhabited Colorado: the Ute, the Shoshone, the Snake, the Navajo, the Arapahoe, the Comanche, and the Kiowa. All of these issues and pressures of the office were secondary to Gilpin's commitment to prevent Colorado's secession from the Union.

Gilpin recognized the importance of gold in the Colorado mountains and that the miners were strong supporters of the Southerners' cause. He also was aware that the Confederacy would try to conquer the territory for its vast mineral deposits as well as its strategic location. The mines could build and equip the Confederate Army, and a minimum contingency of soldiers could cut off the wealth of Utah, Nevada, Oregon, and California from the Union. Because of Gilpin's strong beliefs, as well as his background as a military officer who had served in the Mexican-American War, he knew that quick decisions must be made concerning the emergencies that now faced him.

CHAPTER 58
THE CALL TO DUTY

Michael's loyalty was with the Union sympathizers and with the country he had adopted and previously fought for in the Mexican and Indian wars. When word went out that Governor Gilpin needed volunteers to counteract and suppress the developing problems, Michael felt it his duty to volunteer, but he knew he needed to discuss the matter with Philomene first.

It was impossible for her to say or do anything that would keep Michael from following his dreams to give back to a country that had unconditionally adopted him.

The 1st Regiment of Colorado Volunteers began enlistment in August 1861 and Michael was in line early to sign up. His enlistment was for a period of 3 years and he would receive $30 a month in the form of a government draft.

Little did these early volunteers know that the funding Gilpin had requested for this new regiment was not forthcoming. Gilpin simply continued the organization of this regiment based on his belief that it was critical to the Union's survival in this new Colorado Territory. He continued to issue drafts directly on the United States in order to meet the necessary expenses of supplying this organization and equipping the men with necessary items. To supplement the immediate need for arms, he sent out his staff to buy and collect all the arms they could get. This not only helped to supply needed arms to the troops but would also keep the arms out of the hands of Southern sympathizers.

Private Michael Myers was assigned to Camp Weld, just outside the Denver City boundaries. Philomene and his daughters accompanied him, and Philomene was immediately welcomed into the medical staff that was formed.

Denver City, having been founded in 1858 under the leadership of Southerners, still held the edge in the community. Now these sympathizers began congregating in various locations to plan support of Confederate troops. One plan uncovered was to take Fort Garland in the southern part of this new territory, capture the artillery there, and go to Texas to fight for the rebel cause. As authorities became aware of this, the newly formed troops began searching the area for such rebel strongholds. As troops from both Fort Lyons and Fort Weld began their patrols along the base of the mountains outside Denver City, the rebels became apprehensive and soon quietly scattered.

The second assignment of the Colorado Volunteers was to intercept and capture a group of forty Southern sympathizers that was being led by a former Texas Ranger. The prisoners were all placed in the Denver City jail and became troublesome for both the townspeople and the authorities.

In late fall, new volunteers were mustered into Federal Service at Camp Weld under the command of Major John Chivington. In February 1862 the volunteered troops marched from Camp Weld to Fort Union in northern New Mexico and on to Glorieta Pass. This forced march covered 400 miles in 14 days over Raton Pass in intense cold and deep snow. Combat commenced shortly after their arrival on the battlefield, leaving them little time to recuperate.

The rebels dreamed of access to the Santa Fe Trail and the gold mines of Colorado. They dreamed of changing the course of the war and fulfilling their destiny. The Union Army knew they had to deny the realization of these dreams. So then, in the westernmost campaign of the Civil War, about 3,000 soldiers on each side engaged in battle. The Confederacy won most tactical victories but the Colorado Volunteers, made up of harsh countryside and determined men, won out and forced them to return to Texas empty-handed. More than 280 Confederate troops died there with their dreams.

CHAPTER 59
FORT GARLAND ADVENTURES

The infantry units were converted to cavalry units and became the First Colorado Cavalry Volunteers and were sent to posts and camps throughout the territory to hold check the hostile Indians. Michael was sent to Fort Garland in the San Luis Valley of southern Colorado Territory, about 300 miles north of Fort Union.

Philomene and the family soon joined him there and, in keeping with the rules, had to find lodging outside the fort itself. This did not deter Philomene. Based on her past medical experience, she quickly found employment with the post hospital. The sanitary conditions were primitive throughout the fort and even at the hospital. Her work was cut out for her and required immediate attention. Caring for her daughters and her work schedule, her life left little extra time for enjoyment.

The First Colorado Volunteers, under Lieutenant Edward A. Jacobs, were to be retained in federal service pending the return of regular troops to maintain this western frontier outpost. Although there had been no Indian issues near the fort, after a short visit to the fort by Colonel Chivington, brief expeditions were sent into the surrounding mountains and valleys to maintain the peace.

The soldiers at Fort Garland were to play another critical role in preserving the West for the Union. Beginning in March 1863, people in the nearby mountains and the San Luis Valley were being murdered for no explainable reason. The bodies were also being mutilated. Finally after one such attack, one person was able to escape and identify the killers. Felipe Espinosa, his brother, and a cousin, were carrying out the murders to avenge the deaths of relatives during the Mexican-American War and because they felt that their lands, which were Spanish land grants recognized by the U.S. government, were stolen or squatted on illegally.

Fort Garland soldiers went on the hunt for the Espinosas, but their efforts proved unsuccessful until the commanding officer at Fort Garland recruited Tom Tobin, who had unusual abilities as a trapper, scout, fighter, and bounty hunter. Tobin set out with a detachment of one officer and fifteen soldiers. Michael Myers was one of this detachment. The fourth day out Tobin found the three bandits, slew them, cut off their heads, and placed them in a sack. Back at the fort, he threw the heads from the sack onto the ground at the colonel's feet. Thus ended the bloody trail of the Espinosas, who killed at least thirty men. Those heads were taken to Denver and during an intermission at the recently built Tabor Opera House, the heads were dramatically rolled across the stage as the audience gasped in horror.

New federal troops began to arrive to relieve the Colorado Volunteers, but in the army's many ironies, these new soldiers tasked with securing Colorado for primarily white Anglo settlements, were a diverse lot. Most were foreign-born, including many Germans, and many could speak no English. Michael, with his command of both English and German, became invaluable to the officers of the fort. His service continued to be required until the spring of 1864 when his enlistment was up. He and his family were returned to Camp Weld, outside Denver City, and Michael was discharged from his service.

CHAPTER 60
HOMESTEADING

On their arrival in Denver City in 1864, Michael and Philomene found it bustling with activity and becoming more crowded with new arrivals each day. This was far from their expectations or their desires for peace and freedom.

While the gold and silver mania was partially responsible for this amazing growth, the Homestead Act of 1862 was creating a different excitement. This federal law gave an applicant ownership of land, typically called a "homestead," at little or no cost. It gave settlers 160 acres. It had been enacted as an expression of the "Free Soil" policy of Northerners who wanted individual farmers to own and operate their own farms, as opposed to Southern slave-owners who wanted to buy up large tracts of land and use slave labor, thereby shutting out free white men. Under this act, any adult who had never taken up arms against the U.S. government could apply. Women, blacks, and immigrants were eligible.

As Michael and Philomene became more aware of the Homestead Act, Michael, especially, thought it possible his earlier dreams of freedom could now become a reality. Land that he could call his own. Fresh air to breathe and calmness away from the hustle and bustle of many of the other places he and his family had lived.

As they considered where to homestead, one area kept coming up for further review. It was a place they had passed through on their original wagon trip to Denver: the Bijou River valley southeast of Denver City. This was where the wagon train had encountered hungry Indians and had found them exceptionally friendly. The surrounding low hills sprouted evergreen trees, which added to the attractiveness of the area. This seemed the best choice and not too far from the civilized world. Michael planned to ride out to make sure their memory had been correct and if so, stake the property as required by the Homestead Act and file a claim for it in Denver.

At no cost, he acquired the land of their dreams. Michael's thoughts turned to his youth and his parents and their struggle for survival on the small portion of land in Germany that they farmed but did not own.

Michael wasted no time. He acquired a wagon, loaded it with necessary provisions and lumber. The next morning, they set off on this new adventure, along with their three daughters. The oldest, Caroline, was now 13 years old.

CHAPTER 61
HOMESTEAD LIVING

A sod cabin was soon built with Philomene's help and occasional help from other nearby homesteaders. While the living quarters were cramped and nothing like they were accustomed to, they handled their close quarters with happiness and good will. The younger daughters took daily care of the chickens and milk cow. The oldest daughter, Caroline, helped Philomene with the cooking and other duties of the household.

As time passed, the family noticed a few Indians gathered on a nearby hill watching their daily actions. The Indians watched the younger girls comb each other's hair, feed the chickens, and romp around the area surrounding the sod home. Perhaps the Indians were trying to determine how their own lives would be affected by this new intrusion.

One afternoon while Philomene and Caroline were baking cookies in their small oven, Caroline observed excitement by the Indians as they were apparently gathering the smell of the baking to their noses. As the first cookies came out of the oven, Philomene, on an impulse, put a few in her apron and went out the door and slowly approached the Indians.

Holding the cookies carefully in her apron with one hand, she gave the Indian friendship sign with the other and spoke the Indian words Michael had taught her for friend, "Chick a son." She handed a cookie to each of the Indians. Each carefully examined and smelled it. Philomene took a bite of one of the cookies and smiled as she chewed it. The Indians looked at each other, then, likewise, carefully raised the cookies to their mouths and took a small bite. As they swallowed, they smiled and jabbered in Indian language to each other. Philomene waved her hand, turned her back, and walked happily back to the cabin.

At dinner that night, Caroline related her mother's actions with the Indians. At first Michael showed concern that Philomene would risk her safety in such a manner, but then reconsidered and praised her for her action. He had learned from past experiences that friendliness always wins out.

Philomene's action was repeated many times in the next

weeks and months. Many times Caroline alone would perform the ceremony. Word spread, and different groups of Indians would appear, waiting quietly for their "hand out."

All went well until one day, a group of six Indians appeared on an adjacent hill. They watched carefully as the cookie ritual was received by the regular Indian group and at the normal time and place. A few days later, while the sun was overhead, this strange new group appeared at the normal place of exchange but much earlier than the usual time.

As Caroline placed the cookies in her apron to take to this new group, she had a fleeting concern. "Why this concern?" she wondered.

CHAPTER 62
INDIAN PROBLEMS

Caroline's tension rose considerably as she drew nearer to this new group of Indians. They were not smiling on her approach as did the regular Indian group. All her feelings sobered instantly by the frightening possibility that these Indians were not friendly and may wish to harm her.

Her body became rigid with fists clenched as two of the Indians leaped from their horses, grabbed her, and lifted her up to one of the other Indians. Caroline's screaming tore at her throat, as she clawed at her capturer. The screams, heard by her mother watching helplessly at the cabin door, would never be forgotten. The cookies in Caroline's apron were scattered on the ground. It had not been the cookies that these Indians were seeking.

A brave of the friendly Kiowa Indian tribe happened to observe Caroline's capture from the hillside just north of the homestead. He watched carefully and unobserved as the hostile Indians rode off to the south with Caroline. At a safe distance, he followed them to determine where they were taking her. The sun was in the early afternoon sky when the hostile Indians, with their captive, reached their village in a valley of the Dry River.

The friendly Kiowa brave raced to his own village to notify his elders what he had observed. After a short discussion with members of the tribe, the chief determined they must ride to the homestead and offer their assistance in the rescue of the "cookie" girl.

In the meantime, Philomene called Michael in from the field, where he was working, to notify him of the capture and of her dark premonitions and concerns for Caroline if she was not rescued quickly.

Word went out to nearby homesteaders that help was needed, and they immediately responded and gathered at Michael's homestead.

They all recognized how serious Caroline's capture truly was. The peace around the general area of these homesteaders had been greatly disturbed. In November 1864, just 6 weeks earlier, a vicious attack and slaughter by

Colonel Chivington and his 100-day volunteers was conducted on a peaceful Indian village farther southeast on Sand Creek. While the village braves were away on a hunting expedition, their women and children were attacked and almost all were killed. The Cheyenne and Arapaho braves sought revenge. Just a month previously a homesteader's entire family, named Hungate, had been massacred, and only a week ago, Mrs. Dietemann, the wife of one of Michael and Philomene's neighbors had been captured, killed, and scalped. Fear of the unknown knotted and writhed in Michael and Philomene's stomachs as if they had been hit by a thunderbolt.

As Michael was forming his posse, the chief and at least ten Kiowa Indian braves appeared on the south hillside. The other homesteaders were fearful until Michael offered his usual friendship sign and it was returned.

Only then did they approach the group of settlers while holding their trepidation in check. The chief explained in sign language that they were here to help and to let them know they would lead them to the village where Caroline was being held in the valley on Dry Creek. Michael immediately expressed his thanks to the chief and his braves.

As the group rode south following the chief and his braves, Michael drew on his previous military experiences and devised a plan. The sun was lowering in the western sky as they approached their destination. Hidden behind one of the hills near the hostile village, Michael explained his tactical plan to the chief and the others.

Four or five Indians would sneak around to the southernmost hills and await a prearranged signal, by Michael, to show themselves. The group of homesteaders would split up and do likewise on the two northernmost hills. Michael, the chief, and one brave would enter the village with no weapons on them and seek conversation with the leader of these hostile Indians.

All went as planned and a discussion began with the hostile leader. Michael demanded that the leader release their captive, noting that she was his daughter and his village would suffer if his demand was not immediately honored. The hostile Indian leader hesitated and seemed taken back by such demands. To further convince the leader, both

Michael and the chief raised their hands and patted the top of their head, thereby giving the signal for the hidden Kiowa Indians and homesteaders to rise up and surround the village.

Without another word, the hostile leader ordered that Caroline be produced. She ran to her father with open arms and shouts of relief from her nightmare. In an effort to demonstrate peace, the leader touched Caroline's reddish hair in a manner that indicated no harm was intended to this God-like creature who had hair unlike any the tribe had ever seen before.

The chief and Michael signaled to the surrounding hills that all was well. They withdrew from the village leaving the hostile chief in a paroxysm of fear should any future attempts be made on Michael's family or those of his friends.

A party was held at the Myers's homestead the day after Caroline and her father returned home. The Kiowa Indians and the homesteaders joined together to celebrate Caroline's safe return. With an understanding that no "fire water" would be served with Indian guests present, various kinds of cookies were made available, and leftovers were sent home to the village with the Kiowa braves.

As time would have it, Michael and Philomene's daughters blossomed into desirable young ladies, and gentlemen callers seemingly appeared out of nowhere. A young rancher named George Adelbert Wood, age 21, soon won Caroline's favor and when she reached age 16 they were married. The wedding took place at the InterContinental on December 25, 1868, the grandest hotel in Denver.

CHAPTER 63

HONORING THE 5-YEAR TERM

Michael devoted this period of his life to improving his homestead, as required by law to attain full ownership. Accordingly, the homesteader must live on and improve the land for a period of 5 years at which time, on proof of these actions, clear title would be issued. These 5 years would be up in the late spring of 1869.

Farming on the Great Plains was not easy. Settlers quickly realized that the plains did not yield crops as readily as the land in the East. Planting on the plains required deep plowing for moisture, then breaking out the soil surface to catch and hold any precipitation. Dry farming, further, required a heavy reliance on the strength and energy of the settlers themselves. Wheat was generally the crop of choice, but declining prices for a bushel of wheat caused many homesteaders to give up farming and seek their fortunes elsewhere.

Not so with Michael. He toiled long and hard, and with the

help of income from other odd jobs, he and his family survived.

The problem with the Indians had calmed considerably since Caroline's rescue. One exception was the "sport" the younger hostile Cheyenne Indians engaged in as they pursued the recently established Butterfield stage coach as it ran through Michael's property on its way to Denver City. Many times Philomene and the girls would watch as the stage passed a quarter mile away from their cabin with horses at a full run and the Indians closely following, shouting and shooting arrows at the stage coach. Michael had gotten so used to this tactic by the Indians that he didn't even stop working and look up. This had become a frequent event for the Butterfield stage coach on its 4-mile run between Bijou Creek Station and Kiowa Station. Occasionally, the hostiles would chase the stage into the Twenty Mile House, just 20 miles outside Denver City.

Michael received the clear deed to the property and while priding himself with property ownership, he was not content with dry land farming and all the hard work it entailed. On one of his trips into Denver City and after a few drinks with a number of his "old cronies," with whom he had served in the Colorado 1st Volunteer unit, he discovered the army was issuing a special bonus to veterans who had served at Fort Garland. He further learned that he had to travel to Fort Garland to receive this bonus.

Both he and Philomene had enjoyed their time at Fort Garland and the mountain valleys and the fertile land of the San Luis Valley near the fort, so they decided to make the trip.

Their immediate thought was to take the stage to Fort Garland as soon as possible. However two obstacles stood in their way. One was the Colorado winter weather of January 1869. The second was that Caroline had just announced that she was pregnant and needed her mother to act as midwife for the delivery.

Always open to new adventures and solutions for the trials and tribulations of life, Michael and Philomene discussed the alternatives available to them. Mid-April would be an ideal time to start their travel with Caroline to Fort Garland while she was only 4 months pregnant. By all calculations Caroline should be safely able to make the trip with them. This, of course, would take her away from her husband until after the baby with born. This became a major concern for both families. Coupled with this was the problem of what to do with Michael and Philomene's two younger daughters, Margaret and Mollie.

By mid-February Michael had investigated stage coach routes and costs involved for a mid-April trip to Fort Garland. He discovered it would take 5 days of daylight travel for the 200-mile journey. That meant five overnight stops at the various stage stations. Two different stage coach lines would have to be used, which complicated scheduling. The approximate cost would be 7 to 10 cents a mile per passenger depending on the pricing at the time of travel. Additional costs for overnight accommodations and meals would add an estimated $2 per person per day.

Michael concluded the trip would cost somewhere between $24 and $30 each, for a grand total of $72 to $90 for the three of them. Since Michael had always been frugal and had saved "rainy day" money over many years of hard labor, he felt the trip was doable.

The only problem that remained was George Adelbert and whether he would permit Caroline to make the trip.

CHAPTER 64
THE RETURN TO FORT GARLAND

George Adelbert Wood was an ambitious young man with his own homestead and always looking for new opportunities and adventures, much like Michael. George Adelbert recognized that as Denver City became more populated, the suppliers of beef would be able to reap a healthy profit. The problem was little beef was currently available to the growing city.

George and six of his neighbors decided to travel to Texas and bring back the nucleus for future large cattle herds. They knew the war had left ranchers in Texas with several million head of Longhorns that could now be bought cheaply for $4 a head. They figured to take advantage and tap into the lucrative southern market with a little start-up capital and a few months herding the cattle back to Colorado.

The group would leave for Texas in April and be back by September. They planned on buying one bull for every ten heifers and drive them back up the newly established Chisholm Trail. On their return, they would have the option to sell them, at market, for $40 a head or keep them as range and breeding stock.

Consequently, Caroline was now free to go with her parents on the trip to Fort Garland. A neighbor family, the Browns, who had two children of their own, a boy and a girl who were close in age to Michael and Philomene's two daughters, offered to take care of Margaret and Mollie. Once this was settled, no more obstacles stood in the way of their trip to Fort Garland.

Tickets were purchased for seating on the Denver and Santa Fe Stage and Express leaving on April 15, 1870, for the first stage of the travel: Denver to Walsenburg. They would connect to the Cottrill, Vickroy, Barlow, Valle, and Barnum Stage Line at Walsenburg, Colorado for the final part of the trip over La Veta Pass to Fort Garland.

April 15 arrived very quickly and they were up early and off on their new adventure. As they boarded the stage coach, they learned it had rules for the passengers. No smoking while in the coach, no spitting on the floor or out the windows, no swearing if ladies are present, no encroachment on your neighbor's space (especially sleeping on their shoulder), and passengers must, at all times, comply with the driver's instructions.

There would be five overnight stays at home stage stations. Lodging was available but might have limited sleeping space, dirt floors, and meager meals. During daylight, the stage would stop every 12 to 15 miles at a swing station for a 10-minute break to switch the horses if necessary. The home stations would be Castle Rock, Colorado Springs, Pueblo, Walsenburg, and after their transfer to the second stage line, at La Veta. The timing for arrival of this stage was flexible since it was traveling from Bent's Fort on the Santa Fe Trail, 50 or so miles east, through yet hostile Indian country, to Walsenburg. They learned that from the La Veta Home Station to Fort Garland, due to the uphill trip over the pass, the coach would require a six-horse team rather than the usual four-horse team. Other than for a few bumps, bruises, and moments of concern for Caroline and her pregnancy, they arrived healthy and happy at Fort Garland.

CHAPTER 65
THE SUMMER OF 1870

At Fort Garland, Michael found only a few of the soldiers with whom he had previously served. After duty hours, they met at the fort's cantina to share stories over a glass or two of the only available beverage.

Philomene discovered many of the same medical staff at the hospital with whom she had served. She was welcomed enthusiastically and immediately offered a job while staying at the fort. Together, they would be able to watch carefully over Caroline's pregnancy. Philomene accepted without a moment's hesitation and felt a wonderful sense of being home.

With his usual enthusiasm, Michael traversed the land outside the fort for available and desirable homestead land. Day after day and week after week he explored from the east end of the San Luis Valley to the west end and from the mountains in the north to the endless prairie land to the south. All the choice land had already been homesteaded, and he discovered even the second choice land had already been filed on by other veterans or pioneers also seeking new opportunities.

The idea of not finding property in the San Luis Valley to homestead slowly germinated in Michael's mind. A visit to the local recorder's office further convinced him he was too late. He learned that there had only been a limited number of homesteads allotted to the fort's veterans and that they had all now been awarded.

Michael felt that his dreams had been drowned in overpowering circumstances but, then, with a sudden breathless instance of relief, he felt freed and he knew that his future remained with his homestead on the Bijou outside the recent settlement of Kiowa, Colorado Territory.

When Michael entered their cabin that evening after learning these facts, both Philomene and daughter Caroline thought he looked vacant, spent, and all his emotions had been smoothed away. They listened intently, as Michael related what he had learned. The room was silent as the full impact of this information was digested.

Shortly, Philomene verbalized the memories of the happy times on the Bijou and slowly brought Michael back to the reality of their current situation. Caroline's baby will soon be born and her return to Kiowa with the baby should be their main focus. Additionally, Caroline's husband, George Adelbert, would be returning with cattle for their ranch and, undoubtedly, would need Michael's help.

On September 8, 1870, Cora Anna Wood, Caroline's first born, came into the world with Philomene's help as midwife.

As soon as Caroline and the baby could safely travel, they all returned the way they had come just 6 months previously and wiser for the adventure.

CHAPTER 66
BACK TO THE HOMESTEAD

Michael worked the old homestead as before and was happy to be among old friends and family. Philomene and Michael's two younger daughters, Margaret and Mollie, soon married and began families of their own.

Michael added to his property ownership by purchasing surrounding land at $2.50 per acre from other homesteaders moving on to new adventures. By the year 1878, in this manner, he had acquired an additional 480 acres, giving him a full section of 640 total acres. This was much too large for him to properly farm but ideal for cattle grazing. His herd was rather small in comparison to most of the other younger settlers but provided income to sustain him during his loss of energy, stamina, and willpower brought on by his declining years.

As son-in-law George Adelbert Wood's herd began to grow and become too large for the grazing land found on his own ranch, a deal was stuck for George to acquire Michael's full 640 acres. A deal made in heaven, thought Philomene, especially so, in light of Michael's failing health. Michael's stubbornness slowed the decision, but finally the deal was made. This permitted Philomene and Michael to retire to township life in the new settlement of Kiowa only 4 miles north of Caroline and George's bustling ranch.

Philomene would be close enough to continue to be midwife to daughter Caroline and deliver all fifteen additional children Caroline conceived. Sadly, three of these children, all younger than 3 years of age, died in 1892 of diphtheria within a month of each other.

During the following years, Michael's health began to further slow him down, much to his consternation but he still found time to periodically visit the numerous friends he had acquired over the last quarter century. Included in these visits was the old Indian chief who had helped in the rescue of Caroline many years before. On this particular visit, Michael was always sure to have a basket full of Philomene's special cookies.

These visits all came to a halt early in the year 1899.

Michael became home bound and succumbed to his growing health problems on July 29, 1899, at 10:40 a.m. surrounded by nearly all his family.

A wake was held in Kiowa and widely attended while "Grandpa Myers's" still body lay cooling in the covered buck wagon a short distance away, on the lonely road. The next day the funeral was officiated by Rev. Curran of Elizabeth and was one of the largest held in Elbert County.

Although hardened by his adventures of life, the barren prairie, and a period of time in which he showed his bravery and distinction, Michael dream's had been fulfilled. He left behind footprints in the sands and soil of time, not only in Colorado Territory, but in the territory of New Mexico and the states of Kansas, Missouri, Minnesota, Illinois, and Pennsylvania, as well as in his native Germany and the other points served outside the United States of America while in the military service to his adopted country.

The burial took place July 29, 1899, on a sun-swept hill west of the homestead belonging to his daughter Caroline and her husband George Adelbert Wood.

The old Kiowa Indian chieftain, with two of his older braves beside him, stood undetected a short distance from the burial ceremony of Michael. After the attendees at the grave left, the chief solemnly approached the gravesite and slowly walked around it chanting while waving white eagle feathers from the grave to the blue sky ensuring that Michael's spirit, dreams, and guidance be ever present with his children and all the future generations to follow.

THE END

****
****
****
****
**
*

DREAMS

Stir the Magic of Your Dreams to Action...

Then

With a Heart for any Fate
Live Those Dreams to the Fullest !

Made in the USA
Columbia, SC
28 October 2017